SAN JUAN NOIR

SAN JUAN NOIR

EDITED BY MAYRA SANTOS-FEBRES

Translated by Will Vanderhyden

AKASHIC
BOOKS

Published by Akashic Books
©2016 Akashic Books

Series concept by Tim McLoughlin and Johnny Temple
San Juan map by Sohrab Habibion

ISBN: 978-1-61775-296-4
Library of Congress Control Number: 2016935084

First printing

Akashic Books
Twitter: @AkashicBooks
Facebook: AkashicBooks
E-mail: info@akashicbooks.com
Website: www.akashicbooks.com

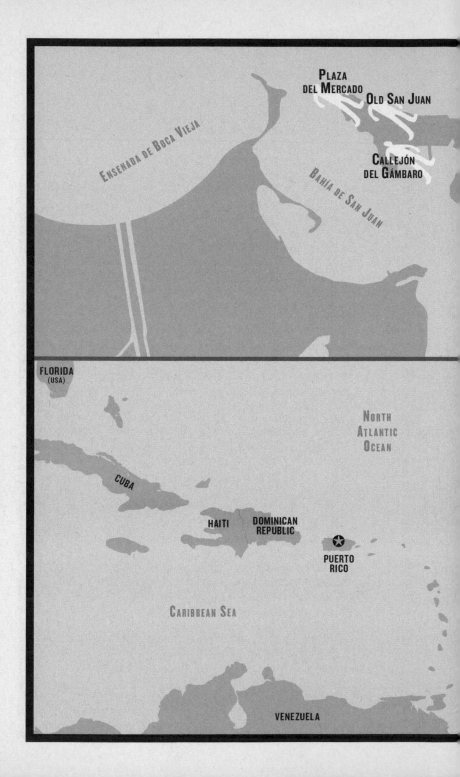

NORTH ATLANTIC OCEAN

DOS HERMANOS BRIDGE

EL CONDADO

AVENIDA FERNANDEZ JUNCOS

TRASTALLERES

SANTURCE

1

2

BARRIO OBRERO

22

HATO REY NORTE

SAN JOSÉ

SAN JUAN

18

SANTA RITA

BUEN CONSEJO

RÍO PIEDRAS

TABLE OF CONTENTS

PART III: NEVER TRUST DESIRE

INTRODUCTION
CRIMES OF THE URBAN CARIBBEAN

Puerto Rico is often portrayed as sandy beaches, casinos, luxury hotels, relaxation, and never-ending pleasure—a place that satisfies all senses and appetites.

Yet the city of San Juan is much more than that. The capital of the Commonwealth of Puerto Rico is the oldest Spanish settlement in all the territories and colonies of the United States. Since Puerto Rico is economically dependent on the US, the financial downturn of 2008 hit us hard. Many Puerto Ricans have left the island, looking for a better life. Crime has risen and the black market has thrived. As in many crises, art, music, and literature have also flourished. Never before has there been so much literary production. We have responded to our crisis with many stories to tell. And, especially in these times, many of those stories are noir.

San Juan's diverse districts include Hato Rey, with both residential and banking buildings; El Condado, with its luxury hotels; and the beautifully kept colonial district of Old San Juan. But between these first world neighborhoods lies an impoverished and dangerous city. The dilapidated streets of the once prosperous Río Piedras are filled with old Spanish Revival quintas that have been converted—some into bars, others into homeless shelters for immigrants and sex workers. Avenida Gándara and Avenida Ponce de León, major commercial arteries during the fifties and sixties, now act as gateways to this decaying area. Barrio Obrero, famously a hotbed for salsa music, is now controlled by the drug trade. If you follow Avenida Borinquen to Laguna San José, through Buen Consejo, Cantera, and Residencial las Margarita, you can watch as small boats loaded with drugs arrive, guided by former fishermen. Inland, nestled in lush, green hills, Caimito and other nearby barrios attempt to create distance from the violence of the city.

This anthology gathers stories that take place all over San Juan, in both the poorest and richest neighborhoods. The first section, Fallen Angels, opens with "Death on the Scaffold." Author Janette Becerra sets her story in Santa Rita, home of intellectuals, university professors, lawyers, and doctors, who live imprisoned in their high-rise buildings, trying to escape the dangers that surround them. Then we move to Callejón de Gámbaro in Old San Juan with Manolo Núñez Negrón in "Fish Food." This is a tale of friendship between two boys—one poor, the other not so poor, but not rich either. Tere Dávila takes us outside of the gated colonial city and into Barrio Obrero; in "el barrio," the humble, God-fearing janitor Chin Fernández is caught committing the petty crime of stealing women's underwear. Yet this is not the worst of his sins. In "Two Deaths for Ángela," a young woman fights disconnection and loneliness while roaming from Calle Loíza to Calle Canals to Plaza del Mercado de Santurce—all gathering places for salsa dancing, intimacy, and love. The protagonist's perspective is vastly darker, filled with violence, attempted rape, and death. My own story, "Matchmaking," portrays the life of El Koala Gutierréz, a hit man with a dispassionate life. In barrio Buen Consejo, he discovers desire, and it leads to his demise.

Part II: Crazy Love opens with "Dog Killer," a story by the 2014 Lambda Literary Award winner Luis Negrón, the first Puerto Rican to win this prestigious prize. We are guided through Parada 15–18 in Santurce, near Cajellón Colectora, an alley in Trastalleres. This barrio is known for being where salsa singer Andy Montañez grew up. Once prosperous, the factories have now closed, and the area is full of unemployed workers roaming the streets, searching for money. Outside the gates of a shut-down factory, a different kind of love emerges. In "Saint Michael's Sword," one of Puerto Rico's most renowned noir writers, Wilfredo J. Burgos Matos, offers a bewildering story that takes place in Río Piedras, just a few streets away from Hato Rey. His hustler protagonist, Ángel, wakes up injured in the middle of the street and must figure out who attacked him. In "A Killer Among Us," we travel back in space and time to a rural community on the outskirts of the city, where urban development meets the campo where the cane cutters lived. Many of these rural workers left the island and settled in the US, and Manuel A. Meléndez, the son of one of those original emigrants, imagines a life that could have been his. "Sweet Feline" is set in El Condado, the tourist district; Alejandro Álvarez Nieves depicts a hotel worker and call girl, and what goes on behind closed doors in one of the many extravagant hotels on the island. In

"Things Told While Falling" by Yolanda Arroyo Pizarro, the murder of Violeta pulls a detective deep into the passionate love triangle between a husband, his young wife, and her best friend, a lesbian. As the cop delves further into the mystery, he learns that "found bodies make silent speeches."

Part III: Never Trust Desire comprises stories by Ernesto Quiñonez, an Ecuadorian–Puerto Rican writer living in New York; SM de Literatura Juvenil award winner José Rabelo; acclaimed author and digitial communications manager Edmaris Carazo; and poet and short story writer Charlie Vázquez. Quiñonez's beautiful narrative brings the reader across the Don Hermanos Bridge as an expatriate returns in search of his father. His sentimental connection to the city leads him astray, and he is deceived as to his true origins. Next, Rabelo gets inside the head of a math teacher and his desire for Samira, an underprivileged student from the Manuel A. Pérez housing development in Río Piedras. One day Samira disappears, but the paths of the two protagonists eventually cross in the streets of Santurce, and the maestro's forbidden love comes to fruition. Then we travel back across the city to Old San Juan with Edmaris Carazo. She tells of a hit-and-run provoked by drugs and alcohol, in which an ordinary young woman becomes an accessory to the crime: San Juan's violence is pervasive, and can turn anyone into a killer. In the last story, "Death Angel of Santurce," the body of a streetwalker is found on Avenida Fernández Juncos. The police insist that it's an open-and-shut case that should be forgotten. But then the reader is taken back to the hours before the woman's death, when she is desperately seeking love and survival.

These are the stories of *San Juan Noir*. I hope they spark your imagination, and reveal a side of Puerto Rico otherwise obscured by the tourist trade and preconceptions. Maybe it will also pique your curiosity, and you will come visit our "pearl of the Caribbean."

Mayra Santos-Febres
San Juan, Puerto Rico
July 2016

PART I

FALLEN ANGELS

DEATH ON THE SCAFFOLD

BY JANETTE BECERRA

Santa Rita

I was only interested in the incident because I ended up looking him in the eye. I had him up close, so I looked into his eyes. That little gesture, for someone familiar with my proclivities, makes a world of difference. You see, beyond the careful contemplation of what takes place inside my own apartment, I'm blessed not to see. From the height of my apartment, Río Piedras is just a mosaic of sepia tones, with a few tiles for garish contrast scattered here and there. Its grout, cracked and gray, is made up of avenues and alleyways of nervous trajectories, bustling with mechanical insects and organisms of unknown species, walking about day and night with purposes that—for me, at least—remain indecipherable. There, in the distance, the blur of San Juan: an impressionist painting of restless brushstrokes, silver streaks with white dots that I've never been able to identify, and beyond that, the sea. That stripe of cobalt blue they call the ocean, there in the distance. Here, above, none of that matters. I go down once a week to stock up on the essentials. There's a shop on the first floor where I get what I need, which isn't much. The rest of my life transpires between these four walls. Let's call it my private command center. Perhaps the world is preparing for man's return to the primordial cave, from where you can order and pay for everything, think of and resolve everything, win and lose everything—even your life—without ever going down.

And so, at the beginning of this week (Monday, to be precise), I was startled by the presence of a man at my window. I had completely forgotten that they would be painting the condominium. Yes, an assembly had been called. Yes, overages had been approved. Yes, notices had been left under the door. I always consent to the nonsense that others occupy themselves with. Laissez-faire.

I was sitting in my armchair, with my back to the window, which is what I generally do early in the morning. The living room reverberated with one of Haydn's major quartets. It wasn't quite nine yet and I was enjoying the iridescence that radiated on my orchids during their morning sunning. That's why I was surprised by the sudden shadow. When I say sudden I should probably say unexpected, because to be honest, I clearly remember that it was gradual. It was a curious spectacle, more worthy of nature than of man: the rest of the apartment in shadows; a sphere of light, like a tracking bulb, on the flowers; and in the heart of the light, like an inverse sunrise or a celestial body entering an eclipse, a sliver of shadow rising little by little, until it projected itself across the cattleyas. I don't know if you can appreciate the strangeness of that vision—a circle of the absence of light, in the middle of a circle of light, in the middle of half-light. I sat observing this phenomenon with that hypnotic attention we give to something that seems like a delusion or fruit of the imagination, when we know ourselves susceptible to such visions. And I wouldn't have turned around if it hadn't been for the head of the shadow, which at first appeared so perfect that it seemed celestial; as it ascended, it began to reveal a body made of flaps and adornments sprouting out of it. Then I did turn around, and I saw him. He saw me too.

He was just a kid, couldn't have been more than twenty. He was wearing a T-shirt wrapped around his head like a Palestinian kaffiyeh, and over it the crown of earphones that—whatever they were transmitting— had him nodding frenetically, hyperbolically. He startled me—like I said, I admit it—but my reflexes are so slow that I didn't even try to hide what was already, without a doubt, obvious to him, mostly because of the several seconds of advantage he had, watching me from behind.

Then there were a few—I don't know how many— seconds of a sustained and knowing look. He was climb- ing at the speed of a turtle on his motorized scaffold, and pressing the button that activated the mechanism, with nothing else to do as his vertical world slowly as- cended. I remember that when he saw what I was hold- ing in my hand (because his eyes did stray from mine for a moment, a fraction of an instant), he gave a hint of a smile. I suppose you understand what I'm referring to, right? That intention of a smile we sometimes see in the corners of someone's mouth who's definitely not smiling, no, but holding a smile back. Farther back than the lips, even farther inside, perhaps behind the teeth or on the cupola of the pallet, shaped like an arch, waiting for that solitary moment when at last it can peel itself off the roof of the mouth and be pushed out with the tongue, free now. So it was. He saw me and I saw him. It was done.

Tuesday was another thing entirely because it was anticipated. I've never had curtains because at this height, frankly, privacy ceases to be a consideration. But now that for a brief time I'd been exposed to the gaze of an intruder, now that this foreign coexistence with the painter had been initiated, I had to stay shut in my bedroom. Since I don't have stereo equipment in there, I was able to hear the soft screech of the pulleys as the scaffolding ascended. From the threshold of my bedroom's half-open door, I saw him look inside, feigning disinterest at first and then, assuming no one could see him, scrutinizing the interior of my apartment with such intensity that he even made a visor of his hands and stuck his face against the glass—searching. This time he let himself grin, of course, because he thought he was alone. He made some gesture of sarcasm or criticism. And he kept ascending slowly, histrionically, as noon does.

By Wednesday I had an itinerary of his ascents and descents: he went up initially at a quarter to nine; he came down at twelve like clockwork; he went back up after one; and at three, or maybe three thirty, he came down and didn't return until the following day. I deduced that they painted condominiums from top to bottom, and he must have started with the penthouse on Monday, which is two floors above mine. So that day it was time for him to paint my floor. It was a long Wednesday, shut away in my room without music. I had to leave the door ajar, because the living room windows give a clear view to the back of the bedroom. I crossed into the kitchen a few times, of course. I passed by without looking at him and returned with my ice tray. At five after two (I remember because the digital clock on my stereo, which I contemplated nostalgically in its silence, showed the time) I perceived out of the corner of my eye that he was gesturing to me with his hand, like he was waving. I pretended not to have seen him and shut myself in again.

At three o'clock, desperate for the workday to end so I could retake dominion over my house, I positioned myself at the crack in the door to spy on him. The platform of his scaffolding went way beyond the width of my apartment, so there were long periods when I couldn't see his movements. I watched his torso cross in front of one of my windows and disappear behind the adjoining wall, then reemerge in my field of vision. It took him fifteen or twenty more minutes to complete the day's work. Since he tended to place his equipment on a segment of the scaffold outside of my big living room window (the one out of which I had seen him the first time), I was able to observe when he started to get his things ready to go. He sealed the bucket of paint and began to clean his hands with a cloth from the back pocket of his overalls. Instead of focusing on what he was doing, he entertained himself by looking into my empty living room. He smiled through clenched teeth as if remembering, reliving that Monday morning, and peered into every corner his eyes could reach. It'd been like that since Monday: him, just a boy, inhabitant of a still vertical life; us, old residents of horizontal universes, where there was space for our vices to scatter themselves around. Maybe he was too young; now I'm not even sure he was twenty. He still had a desire to *see*, and that's no longer of interest after a certain age.

When he felt satisfied that he had devoured my slice of the world, he returned to his hands. Then I saw him make an expression of disgust, curse, throw the cloth furiously down on the scaffold floor, and look with despair at the fronts and backs of his fingers, which, judging from his rage, had been left more covered in paint than before—probably because he'd used the same cloth too many times. Then, with his elbow he activated a switch that I'd not seen him use yet, and with the same elbow he pressed the button of the motor for a second and pulled back his arm. The scaffold began its automatic descent, while he rubbed his hands against his chest, butt, and thighs, as if determined to soil himself as much as possible.

Not even ten seconds had passed—I barely had time to take three steps into the living room—when I again heard the screech of the pulleys and saw that the painter was returning. I scurried quickly back toward my room and I saw him pass by my floor on his way up. I was surprised, because he should've already finished painting the upper floor the day before. I slipped timidly into the living room and went up to the glass, but my vantage only revealed the bottom of the wooden platform. I opened a window—the windows here are sash windows—and stuck my head out as far as I could, but I didn't see much. A swaying, nothing more. Observed from below, that platform was transformed into an iron curtain, perfect for concealing the intimacies committed by those on top of it (a real advantage over my apartment, I remember thinking). I noted how the mechanism was flanked by metal brackets, cables, cords, and pulleys that stuck out like tentacles from the condominium's rooftop down to the first floor. I closed the window and returned to my observation point behind my cracked bedroom door, resolving not to enter my living room during the day until the scaffold had definitively descended.

Time passed . . . I don't know, maybe five minutes? It seemed like more to me, restless as I was. The unusual silence of my apartment, which was ordinarily submerged in music, heightened my senses. Maybe I imagined sounds. It was after three thirty. At that hour, the world becomes for me a kind of underwater concert, you know? Everything muffled, slow, majestic. I sensed a thumping in the ceiling: vibrations, like drowned thunderclaps, from the floor above me. One here, another there. It happens. It's not rare in a condo, nor did it bother me. I turn on music, and that's that. But that day, in the silence, combined with my anxious waiting, it attracted my attention. I looked around overhead, trying to find the origin of those sounds to decipher their pattern. They weren't sounds that merited alarm, it was just a way to kill time. Eventually the thumps stopped, and yet I remained in suspense a few seconds more, my eyes lost in the smooth ceiling of my bedroom. Then I went back to the observation that mattered most to me: the scaffold's descent. It came down one or two minutes later, and I felt freed from the prison of that day.

I turned on my music at full volume and had a party. You might understand what I mean when I say I had a party. Such was the celebration that I found it necessary to go down to the shop on the first floor an hour later. I entered the elevator and when I pressed the button for the lobby there was a stain on it, something with the opacity and texture of a relief. It seemed strange—not because I tend to focus on that kind of detail, nothing is more foreign to my personality. It made me remember the recent spectacle of the eclipse over the cattleyas. The buttons in elevators are illuminated, right? That circle of light had a half-moon of shadow in its interior, some imperfection that obstructed the glow. It took shape on the left and stole a piece of illumination from the upper part of the G. I stumbled closer and touched it, like a blind person reading Braille. I returned to the back wall of the elevator and reclined my head, humming a Brahms melody. When the doors opened, I bent forward and leaned against the call panel. With the light of the button now off, I could better study the stain. It was a dry streak of grayish or brown paint, nothing more. I scratched it with a fingernail.

Then I went out into the lobby and saw the commotion.

Everyone was congregating around something in front of the building. The lights of I don't know how many police cars and ambulances spun rhythmically in reds and blues, creating a curiously festive air in the twilight. I went inside the shop and asked the clerk at the cash register what had happened. He told me about the painter, shattered on the pavement. I didn't want go over and see the macabre spectacle that everyone seemed to be enjoying right there and then.

The return trip in the elevator was strange: I stood looking again at the button for the lobby, clean of paint this time. I must have cocked my head or made one of those gestures we make when something doesn't fit.

It wasn't until the next morning, sitting at ease in my living room armchair, that everything became clear. I carefully read the news in the online papers: the police were investigating the unfortunate incident of a painter who'd accidentally fallen from his scaffold. I vividly re-membered the kid and I think I even felt bad about his death; at that hour of the morning it's easy for me to feel empathy for the human race. But I imagined him just as I'd known him—sniffing around more than was appro-priate, his hands forming a visor to look inside and judge the depths of other lives, our lives. What could there be on the floor above that would make him return when his workday was already over? What, in the windows above mine, would've awakened his need to look? I fixed my eyes on the ceiling of my apartment, and just so, like an epiphany, I knew. The threads knit themselves together and everything made sense, old things that you don't even know you remember suddenly link together and create a choir, like the four instruments in the Haydn piece.

Early as it was (I think it wasn't even eight yet), and in an outburst of heroism that, given my tendencies, surely wouldn't last past ten, I decided to meddle. I already knew there was nothing of interest in the penthouse.

The spectacle that had captivated the painter was in the apartment just above mine. That boyish voyeur, with his vertical advantage, had served as a periscope between my eyes and the window above. I went up.

I wasn't sure what I would do or say once the door opened. I was impelled by the precarious sense of coexistence that'd begun with that brief, repugnant visual contact between me and the painter. Silly as it seems, he was the closest thing to a neighbor I'd had in my condo building. Someone familiar with my habits would understand.

I knocked one, two, three times. I knew I was being observed through the peephole; I managed to embody a kind of character by concentrating on synchronizing my heartbeats with my blinking. I suppose that this conferred on me the air of a battery-powered doll, innocuous enough that they'd venture to open the door. I had no idea who occupied that apartment: I was there because I needed to scratch the coat of paint with my fingernail. The rest would come later.

The door opened just a few inches, scarcely enough for me to glimpse a pair of eyes peering through the diagonal along the line of the threshold. This was all that was needed for the other to exist in me, as I suppose you might already understand. And those eyes said everything I needed to hear by revealing their dilated smallness, their suspicious turbidity. We were of the same species.

"Hello," I whispered. And I smiled. I remember that I smiled.

"Yes?"

"I'm here on behalf of the committee. We're calling an urgent meeting of all the residents."

"Yes?"

"Because of the incident yesterday."

"Yes?"

"Will you let me come in?" I didn't want to go in. I wouldn't have had the courage to go in. I just wanted to corroborate that he wasn't ready to allow it. Already, for me, it was obvious.

"No. I can't."

"I understand," I said. "We'll be distributing the notice later on today. Have a good day."

I turned around and hurried to the elevator. As I was walking with my back to that door, which had yet to close, I began to evaluate the risk I was taking in the deserted hallway of an unfamiliar floor, vulnerable to the paranoia of someone who probably knew that he'd been found out. Because he *had* been found out, there was no doubt about it. I could feel the heat of his gaze, his terror that was also my own. The elevator took an eternity; I had time to focus on the call button, perfectly clean, as if it had just been polished. Each additional second that passed without hearing that door lock into place threw more fuel on the invisible fire that devoured the distance between us. I never turned around to check, but I know he was about to jump on me and drag me inside his small hell, just like the rest of them.

I didn't wait any longer. I headed to the stairs and ran down like I was running for my life. I locked myself in my apartment and called you, inventing an excuse for you to come, latching the bolts on the windows, dragging furniture in front of the door, and arming myself with kitchen knives.

And what I want to tell you is that the dry thumps were not just from yesterday. They've been there for months, I don't know, maybe years. This morning, as I was reading the newspaper, a simple truth that I never cared to know became clear to me: my habit of playing music at such a high volume began because I preferred not to hear, not to see. I think I've already told you that I consent to all the nonsense that others do and say laissez-faire. But it's not just thumps, you know? Sometimes there are moans, muffled and choked cries, and heavy round blows that reverberate across the pentagram of my bedroom ceiling. Have you heard the sounds a gagged mouth makes? That sound. A lot of that, sometimes. Mostly before, recently not so much. But yesterday . . . yesterday again, so much! As if the eyes of those silenced mouths had been waiting for the miracle of seeing their redeemer ascending, only to witness his useless expiation.

No doubt the painter saw what he shouldn't have seen. And he was seen looking. Perhaps what he saw—which he must have seen Monday or Tuesday—ended up unsettling or exciting him so much that he wanted to go back up and enjoy it again yesterday, despite the fact that nothing justified his presence there anymore. I bet the apartment above doesn't have curtains. I bet the door to the bedroom is open, because at this height, frankly, privacy ceases to be a consideration.

And now I understand why the scaffolding came down empty at three thirty. Yesterday, I assumed the painter had moved to a segment outside my line of vision, but really he'd already been thrown off. His body must have fallen in the brief lapse when I was distracted by the ceiling and the noises. The killer only had to go out through the window, climb onto the platform, and struggle with him—and in that hand-to-hand struggle, taking into account the paint-covered overalls, it was inevitable that his hands would get dirty. That was the plot point from which I began to deduce everything: the paint stain on the elevator button. He must have gone down right away to pretend to just be part of the crowd that surrounded the body, don't you think? And we must admit that it was a good idea to take care of putting the scaffold in motion. Why call attention to his floor by leaving the platform there, so that later on you would come and examine it? Isn't it better to make the things of this world fall, according to their own weight, while here above you can order and pay for everything, think of and resolve everything, win and lose everything—even your life—without ever going down?

FISH FOOD

BY MANOLO NÚÑEZ NEGRÓN

Callejón del Gámbaro

When we were little we were like dirt and fingernail, that's why it hurt so much. He grew up on Calle Baja Matadero, next to the Placita, and I grew up in one of the houses on the boulevard heading up toward Castillo San Cristóbal. He was fatherless, and in this we were the same. His had been killed at a cockfight, two stab wounds, and mine ran off with a hairdresser, or died in the Gulf War, or got a life sentence in federal prison, it's all the same in any case. I remember because we were celebrating my birthday in front of Castillo del Morro, and Repollo was standing at the base of the wall feeding out string to his kite, which flew much higher than the one my uncle and aunt had given me. At one point I saw him heading down the hill toward the field, driven by my neighbors' dogs, who pulled on the leash like horses, and I was jealous of his luck: he could go to the beach without asking permission, and to Recodo, Tite's Bar, to play pinball. Later on when we were teenagers, he confessed that he would've given anything to live where I did; that it made him sad to see me sitting on the balcony, through the ornamental bars, with a coloring book on my knees. He longed to climb up, run through the city, put on tennis shoes, and get to know the stores full of tourists; I wanted to go down, out to the sea, roll around in the sand, and walk through the slums wearing sandals. Maybe that's why we became such good friends.

My mom was opposed from the start. "Those people are like cats," she said, "they bite the hand that feeds them." She ruled him out from the beginning, and there was no way to convince her that, deep down, he had a good heart. I imagine that she never forgave him for how, after we invited him to the party and gave him a piece of cake, he cut my kite string—which was lost in the sky and traveled on through the air, past the rum factory, searching for El Cañuelo on Isla de Cabras. It didn't bother me. To the contrary, it made me happy, because flying a kite seemed like a game for little girls.

I ran into him again one morning beside the Capilla del Cristo. It was his favorite spot—not because he loved the doves, he actually loathed them—but because from there he could study the arrival of the cruise ships, the chaos of the docks, the small boats crossing the bay. At first I tried to talk to him, offering him a bag of roasted peanuts, and still he reacted indifferently, picking his nose. It was, I think, the first time I noticed his features. His skin was tanned from the sun, his eyes were damp, his forehead broad. A bruise ran across his cheek, graz-ing his lower lip, and more bruises were visible on his neck. At first I was curious and then I felt bad. It's pos-sible that at that moment, inside of me, like a plant left without water, innocence began to die. To earn his trust I bought him a malt and some plantain chips. To tell the truth, I guess that behind his shy character and surly manners there was a spiderweb of insecurity. Childhood is a cruel time. Nothing is worse than a kid alone at recess—I say this with firsthand knowledge. Decades have passed, that environment has receded, and yet, looking at myself in the mirror every morning, holding my razor, my hair graying, I can hear my classmates shouting from the second floor balcony: *Faggot, faggot, faggot!*

He didn't thank me, but he let me sit beside him. He waited awhile in silence, lost in thought, tears of courage rolling down his dirty cheekbones. Both of us, in a way, felt the summer suffocating the flowers, warming the tops of cars, melting caramels in glass jars.

"My mom hit me with a belt," he said.

"Moms are like that," I responded.

After a couple hours we got soaked by a downpour. We made little boats out of paper and launched them into the inlet ditches until it stopped. The rain had a virtue: it imposed a sense of cleanliness, of pulchritude, a new world springing up from the asphalt. We separated in front of Iglesia San Francisco. From that day on he was my accomplice. We went to different schools, it's true, but we saw each other frequently. As we grew up and began to have more freedom, we became closer. We had, of course, some disagreements typical of that age. Standard stuff: trivial fights over a baseball card, a toy pistol, a couple of marbles. He cheated at everything— marked playing cards, hid dominoes, altered dice—but, to my surprise, he avoided these little tricks with me. As an adult, I understood that they were survival tactics: he moved in a universe governed by different rules.

Honestly, in terms of tastes, we were polar opposites. He declared himself cocolo, a fan of the Cowboys, and a lover of McDonald's hamburgers. I, on the other hand, was into rock music, burritos from Taco Bell, and Raymond Dalmau's jump shots. If I said Menudo, he answered Los Chicos; if he suggested Lourdes Chacón, I said Iris, and on and on. I guess we really loved the same things and the rivalry was nothing more than a front. Harmless entertainment that reinforced the ties that bound us together. He never mentioned the incidents with his mother again even though it was clearly a common practice. In the end, he let her hit him and didn't talk back. Human beings adapt to everything. And yet I know he was unable to abolish the beatings from his memory. There are events that remain recorded under the skin, stuck to the bones, and nothing can be done to erase them. It doesn't even do any good to talk about them, because little by little they dissolve, mixing into everything we do. At the smallest provocation, the slightest gesture, it's like a puppet master pulls these events out of a trunk and they come back from the emptiness, and on our faces is an expression of incomprehension, absorbed and disbelieving. Something similar happened to us with the death of Vigoreaux and the DuPont Plaza fire: those events continued to live on in our imaginations, feeding on fear and foreboding.

He gave me my first porn magazine, wrapped in a B&B case. On the cover was a blonde dressed as a nurse. I stashed it away, like a relic, and it probably is. The process, before, had its charm: nudity transmitted an aura of mystery, and it was a marvel hiding away in my room, flipping through the pages, delving into the intimacy of a stranger, feeling the texture of the glossy pages between damp fingers, looking at bodies opening the doors to eroticism and pleasure. Now everyone bends over and shows it all. "We macho machos buy *Hustler*," he warned me. "Pendejos settle for *Playboy*." That observation made such an impression on me that, even today, flipping through such magazines on a shelf in a 7-Eleven, his comment still seems valid. In effect, he was more precocious than I was. At fifteen, his relatives took him to Black Angus, to pop his cherry, and a few months later he passed this kindness to me. "Just stay calm, big guy, she knows what she's doing." It was the best advice I could've gotten, and I repeated it to myself out loud, walking down the long, dark hallway, trembling with excitement and terror.

I rolled him his first joint one Palm Sunday, when we were about to finish high school. He got hooked on weed and almost failed the semester. Well, to be honest, he didn't pass: the teachers came to an agreement and inflated his grades to get him out of there. And that's what he did—he hitched up his gown, walked at graduation, and the next week he joined the National Guard Reserve. He came back from Fort Jackson off his rocker, jacked, his biceps bursting out of his T-shirt, hell-bent on banging all the girls. As soon as he could, he got himself a motorbike, a brand-new Yamaha RX, which he crashed into a wall at Parada 26 coming out of a Palma Party rally. Even in this respect we were different. His family was blue, true blue, and mine was red to the core. We barely ever talked politics, preferring to avoid unnecessary disputes. Things like that sow discord where there is none. I knew that a flag of the ex-governor hung from his window, and that was more than enough.

We grew apart while I was at university, but we still saw each other every now and then. We bumped into each other at Boricua or Ocho de Blanco, dives we went to on the hunt: hair slicked back à la John Travolta, starched and unbuttoned guayaberas, faded blue jeans, riding boots shined to perfection. That was when he started getting into cocaine. He came out of the bathrooms with dilated pupils and a numb jaw, euphoric. He avoided me under these circumstances, ashamed, even though he knew drugs weren't foreign to me and that I'd tried everything—even LSD and hashish, of which I was an aficionado for a time. I found out from other friends, randomly, that he was getting heavily into smack. "He's turning into a junkie," they said. Alone, I cried, I admit it. Nobody returns from that trip intact: they want to come back, get back to the shore, save themselves from the tide that's sucking them out. They fail. A dense jungle, darkness, live ash, snake-bitten shadows, hunting, inexorable. Only the grave frees them from that prison. When I graduated, just scraping by, with a degree in accounting, and with the strike calming down at the university, I lost sight of him. What I mean to say is I stopped seeing him, although not so much his doubles, that multitude of creatures wandering along the avenues and sidewalks: the plastic cup in their ulcerated hands, their breath broken with thirst, happiness fading from their expressions, slow and without rhythm.

And one day around Callejón del Gámbaro, I ran into him when I was coming out of work. He looked stooped, older. He asked for a peso, making it sound like a joke, and I invited him to get a beer. We went into one of those bars on San Sebastián and settled in at the counter, which was covered with candles and ashtrays. He drank calmly, serenely, detached from what was going on behind him at the restaurant tables. He held the bottle with a napkin, and when he brought it to his mouth, foam sliding out the corners, his expression was transfigured. I had the impression that the alcohol ran swiftly through his veins, one by one healing all his wounds. We talked for hours without stopping, laughing loudly. It was very late when we drunkenly said goodbye and I gave him twenty dollars. I heard he got by as a handyman, fixing plumbing and household appliances, but it's possible that he was already involved in other business. Maintaining a vice costs you a nut. Sometimes both.

He disappeared completely around Christmas. The radio played "La Finquita," the hit by Tavín Pumarejo, and also a song by Tony Croato that depressed me: the story of a kid with torn shorts, barefoot and freezing. Repollo didn't leave a trace. Someone told me it was rumored that he'd screwed someone over and taken off. I believed it, so he was either dead or on the run—six feet under, wrapped in a Glad bag, or in an apartment on the Lower East Side, sleeping on a cot, dressed like a janitor. One night, in the middle of a City Council meeting, my doubts were eliminated. Doña Cambucha, the spinster of San Justo, accused him of robbing the rearview mirrors from cars. Can, the girl from Tetuán, seconded the complaint, adjusting her cleavage: "He took the hubcaps off my Nissan, the crook."

I knew right away that his hours were numbered. I searched high and low to find him.

"You're heating up," I warned him.

He smiled, showing his teeth, indifferent, and took a wooden top out of his pocket. He wound the string around the tip, tightening it with his thumb, and threw it onto the ground. That slow dance across the stones entranced us; we were captured by its spinning, tied to its movement; the lost murmur of our innocence, the sounds of the waves crashing against the rocks on the coast, our broken dreams. Immobilized on the benches of the dock, sheltered by a tree, we scrutinized the horizon, the wind shaking the bushes. Hiding my anxiety, I tried to find cracks in his face, signals that would help me guess what was convulsing inside him. I found no answer, just a sad question in his gaze.

"Keep it," he chided, "see if you can learn how to use it."

He headed for Covadonga, prowled around the area, and his pilgrimage ended around the bus station, slouched on a sidewalk, watching the flow of passersby.

Word got around among the neighborhood residents that he'd already been given a warning: "Pickpockets have to go to Condado." It was the logical move. Robberies attract the police, inconvenience the residents, create a climate of suspicion and rancor, and, in the end, damage the drug trade. The important thing is to guarantee the normal flow of goods and services. The recipe is simple: if something alters the social harmony, it's eliminated. So a good capo, apart from being invisible and feared by his peers, insures that there's order. He intimidates thieves, gives the belt to abusers, compensates widows, takes care of appearances, and administers justice. In a sentence: he imposes his law, with an Uzi SMG hanging from his shoulder. There's no other way for the gang to gain ground. I once heard a taxi driver near Tapia say that we need fewer governors and more gangsters.

Life continued on its way. I forgot about the thing with Repollo. My work routine imposed itself against my will. Getting up at six to avoid traffic. Tying my tie, driving to the office. Punching in before eight, taking a break at ten. Eating lunch, filling out forms, attending meetings. Drinking coffee, smoking, snacking on donuts. Monday to Friday: the automation reflected on the computer screen. I was waiting for the bell, and my existence turned into a silent movie.

One day, near the end of my Semana Santa vacation, I was heading up to Hooters when I noticed a crowd gathering around one of the watchtowers, including some police officers and reporters. A soft breeze blew, dragging in an intense, salty odor. I went over to see what was going on, removing my hat, and from a distance I made out the sailboat retrieving a solitary swollen arm, floating out to sea, chewed on by fish.

"It must be from a Dominican," someone speculated. I moved away silently, heartbeats pounding in my chest, sweat running down my thighs. My soul made a junkyard of words, convinced they were wrong. The robberies in the area had stopped, and I hadn't seen him standing on the corner of Ballajá lately, absently peering out of the graveyard. I went out and looked for him everywhere, I must confess, aware of his fate and of the futility of my effort, the top he'd given me clenched in my fist, dancing inside me, inaudible. It's hard to know what his last minutes were like. He was impulsive and antisocial. Brave with little effort. I just hope that they killed him before cutting off his limbs, to spare him the pain. But hired thugs tend to be sadistic, and they have their methods. There's no way to know.

THE INFAMY OF CHIN FERNÁNDEZ

BY TERE DÁVILA

Barrio Obrero

"Invisibility!" he commands, like a superhero from an action comic. But he humbly prays for it from the Almighty too. Chin Fernández asks for the protection necessary to enter the neighbor's patio, cross behind the plantain trees, slip between the trash bins, and make it to the clothesline, where the sheets that were left out all night will provide him the necessary cover on that patio—which is foreign to him, but identical to his own and to all the others in the neighborhood: a narrow U bordering a squat, sweltering house. That familiarity helps him feel less like a scoundrel than he should, crouching behind the three-foot cement wall that separates one residence from the other. There, Chin waits, ready to jump.

The neighborhood is still asleep—Maritza too, Chin is used to getting up and dressing without waking her—as the sky turns from black to violet, and the shapes of things start to emerge. Not a soul in the street, or nearly, because suddenly there's another presence on the pavement. Chin almost jumps from fright, but it turns out to be Prieto, who won't give him away. Better than that, it's good that he's out and about and was able to escape again from Angelito; hopefully he'll get away for good, disappear; but when the dog, recognizing him, comes over, weakly wagging his tail, Chin notices that he's been beaten and maimed, in such pain that he won't be going anywhere. *What kind of person abuses their own animal like that?* he wonders, remembering the afternoon he found him bleeding in an alley.

"Don't bring that dog in the house!" Maritza had scolded him when she saw them approaching.

"But look what that thug did to him . . ."

Maritza shook her head, making it clear that, as usual, Chin didn't understand anything. "Aha, and what will you do when Angelito finds out where his dog is? I don't want that madman showing up here."

She had a point. The next day, Angelito had shown up looking for him.

"Give him back," he said to Chin, one foot inside the house, poisoning everything with his bad blood and demonic appearance: face like a skinhead, skinny as a cable, veins protruding from his neck; like one of those guys who smile just before stabbing you.

"Why don't you leave him with me?" Chin had responded, but the request lacked conviction, like when you ask for a privilege that you know beforehand won't be granted.

"If I see you with my dog again, I'll kill you," Angelito had threatened before taking Prieto away on a chain leash.

Most men named "Angelito" come out just the opposite, Chin thinks, and then fantasizes, with more than a little pleasure, that the guy falls down dead, that someone burns him with the same cigarettes he uses to torture

Prieto, that *he* gets a beating instead off doling them out . . . but no—better to remove bad thoughts from his head. According to the reverend, we sin not just in action but also in thought and, considering where he is now, it would be better to keep his thoughts pure, so God won't abandon him.

Invisibility, he repeats to himself. It's a matter of jumping over, running to the far side of the patio without being caught, grabbing what he wants—he saw it yesterday when the neighbor came out to hang up the clothes—and returning quickly to the street. He feels his heart beating so fast that it's difficult to breath.

I can't handle this kind of stress anymore; lots of forty-year-old men kick the bucket for less.

On the bus heading to work, he keeps his hand in the pocket of his handyman jumpsuit. He punches in. Pours coffee. Cleans the bronze banisters in the lobby where his coworkers hurry by. He eats lunch alone in the cafeteria. And all day long, his hand going in and out of his pocket, stroking his treasure every five minutes: he plans how he'll care for them, how he'll give the stolen panties the value and importance they deserve.

"Can you change Gómez's lightbulb?" says the receptionist, pulling him out of his daydream. And there goes Chin with his screwdriver. Gómez doesn't even greet him or stand up from his desk; he just moves his ergonomic chair to one side so Chin can do his thing without getting in the way.

Where would she look for them? Chin imagines his neighbor looking through drawers, closets, and inside the washing machine, searching for the panties. But she won't find them. Chin smiles and gives his pocket a little pat, thinking about the other women, the previous women, looking for their missing garments; some that must have been their favorites, others that they almost never used, but were reserved for special occasions and for that reason, perhaps, they miss them even more. Because that's the point: they belonged to someone. It's no good to go to a department store and buy a dozen pairs with no history. That someone misses them is precisely what gives them value.

He punches out at six and is on his way, running late, to the church, where everyone is already sitting—Maritza, in the tenth row, hasn't saved him a seat—so he listens to the sermon, which is quite long, standing in the back. When the service is over, he heads to the dais, where the reverend is talking to a few congregants. Normally he avoids greeting him, his wife does that, but considering that morning's activities, he feels the need to earn some points with God.

He waits his turn, looking for a pause in the conversation to greet the reverend, but no one gives him a chance; someone jumps in front of him, or someone else cuts in with another question. So there he is, in front of everyone, his nose buried in chitchat, nobody noticing him, like they don't even see him. He wonders if he really has become invisible; so he gives up and goes back Maritza.

"And that outfit?" she asks, definitely seeing him, or really just his jumpsuit.

She's right, he should've changed. Chin starts to explain: he got held up in the office, he didn't want to be even later—but Maritza doesn't listen, she's busy doling out kisses.

He heads home alone. There's no moon, and Barrio Obrero looks gray and monotone without the color of the day, when the sun strikes the blue, green, pink, and yellow walls of structures that, though identical in construction, show their individuality in layers of paint. Peach, guava, and turquoise—shades more appropriate for lingerie than for concrete.

Chin rubs the stolen panties as if they are a good luck charm. A pair of tennis shoes hangs from a power line.

Angelito. Those shoes must indicate a drug corner that he controls. Or maybe they killed someone there, because when someone gets taken out they say that the dude *hung up his shoes.* Either way it's unclear; Chin doesn't know if they indicate territory or are giving a more serious warning, and anyway, he doesn't know how long they've been there nor who they belonged to. He keeps stroking the little piece of satin; he's almost halfway home when he hears the whimpers.

Prieto.

He goes down an alley to his right, slips behind an abandoned shed, and peers—for the second time in less than twenty-four hours—into someone else's patio, though he'd never wanted to come to this one, nor had he ever been invited.

Chin sees the silhouettes of Angelito and Prieto

against the back wall. The dog curls in on himself, trying to make himself small and disappear, but the boot hits home anyway. Another whimper. Angelito takes a drag from his cigarette—the orange tip glows in the darkness—then exhales, grips the chain that holds Prieto, and extinguishes the coal on his head.

Chin shouts.

"Who's there?" Angelito grunts.

Chin covers his mouth, as if that could cancel the sound. His feet have ignored the order from his brain to take off running; if he goes now, that madman will kill Prieto for sure. Instead, he holds his breath and prays, crouching down being the wall, barely three feet high.

"Come out, cabrón!" Angelito shouts, advancing.

Click.

A knife flicks open in Angelito's right hand. Chin instinctively brings his hands to his pockets, searching for a weapon he knows doesn't exist.

Something, something . . . His right fist closes around an unexpected object: not the piece of satin he's been caressing all day, but something else—the screwdriver that he used to install Gómez's lightbulb.

Barrio Obrero seems bigger than it is. The connected buildings, the many little houses, the daytime activity, all the businesses and small shops bewilder those who don't know the area, but you can walk its perimeter fairly quickly. From Angelito's patio to Chin's house is no more than ten minutes, although right now Chin feels that each step takes forever; he'll never be able to get away from that damned patio. The scene repeats in his mind and he sees again how Angelito falls to the ground, with that skinhead smile turning bit by bit into an incredulous expression—so certain was he that Chin was harmless—with the screwdriver protruding from his neck. The move took him by surprise, he fell to the side and bled out from his throat. Before taking off, Chin let Prieto off his chain. The dog approached the man who until that moment had been his master, and, to check that he was dead, began to lick the bloodied ground.

The street is calm. Nobody has come out, no light has been turned on to signal an alarm, the evening is just like any other. Chin Fernández has gone unnoticed as always. *And what isn't seen here doesn't exist*, he tells himself, turning the corner onto his street.

"Here he comes!" someone announces.

There's a mess of people in front of his house, and worse—two officers, one short and older, the other tall and young, waiting beside a patrol car that looks like a mobile dance club with all its spinning lights.

"Are you Adalberto Jesús Fernández?" asks the older officer.

Chin nods and the younger officer produces a piece of paper that he puts in front of his nose, apparently granting them permission to come inside.

How did they find out so fast?

He doesn't understand. He just left Angelito's patio, nobody saw him, and besides, the police are never that efficient.

He goes upstairs with the two officers, takes out his key to the front door, and looks at his hands. They're clean—he'd found a spigot in the alley—and his old jumpsuit doesn't have any stains that stand out among the others, from oil and paint.

"You take the living room and I'll start in the kitchen," one officer says to the other. Within minutes they go through the kitchen cabinets and the sofa and chair cushions; they take the Sacred Heart down from the wall, and even pull out the TV. They move quickly. They open the doors of the oven and refrigerator, where, of course, they don't find anything of interest, but they leave everything wide open anyway.

Chin, prisoner of panic, covertly feels inside his pockets. *God hasn't forgotten me*, he sighs with relief; only the panties there, he doesn't have the screwdriver on him. He reviews his actions: he definitely removed it from Angelito's neck and threw it away. The police weren't going to find anything.

But meanwhile, they are emptying the medicine cabinet in the bathroom.

"What's all this?" shrieks Maritza, who has just come home from the service. She goes from one officer to the other, ignoring Chin, who wouldn't have known what to tell her anyway. The older officer plants himself in front of her and silences her with a, "Señora, be quiet if you don't want us to arrest you," and that gives her the hiccups.

They move to the bedroom, where they remove all the clothes from the closets and unmake the bed, throwing everything on the floor. Chin, who has remained fixed like a post while the police do their thing, suddenly moves—reflexively, without thinking—to pick up one thing: his pillow. The young police officer sees him and, without giving him a chance to react, rips it away from him. Like a broken piñata, the pillow spits out white, blue, red, pink, black, and violet lace; small pieces of satin and silk, some with bows and little flowers, others with tiger stripes or leopard print.

The police officer bends down and collects the panties, one pair at a time, and starts handing them to his partner. Maritza hiccups and sobs quietly without interrupting the counting process: *seven, eight, nine . . .* and Chin understands at last. Of course someone saw him, but not tonight and not in Angelito's patio. More than anything he's surprised that they view him as someone dangerous.

Seventy-eight, seventy-nine, eighty. That's why the police are there, for the eighty pairs of stolen panties hidden inside the pillow that he, Chin Fernández, has zealously sewn and unsewn for months. The pillow where he rests his head every night.

"Excuse me," he interrupts, "you're missing one."

He takes the panties out of his pocket and, allowing himself the perverse pleasure of breaking the round sum of eighty, he hands them over, so they can be taken into evidence.

The short officer handcuffs him and escorts him, almost courteously, as if he hadn't just destroyed the interior of his house, toward the patrol car, around which more onlookers have gathered. There are the neighbors—including the owner of the patio that Chin infiltrated that morning—the guy who runs the shop two streets down, the reverend, accompanied by some of the church's congregants, and many people who Chin doesn't know who must have come running, attracted by Maritza's screams or by the presence of the patrol car. On the other side of the street, he sees the silhouette of a dog. Prieto? And also an individual with a skinhead's smile who looks a lot like Angelito but who, of course, isn't, because he's wearing the official shirt of Channel 4 News.

"We've got the Barrio Obrero panty-snatcher," the young officer says into his walkie-talkie. "Don't let Rivera leave—we need him to open the file."

And then Chin pictures the screwdriver again. He remembers it disappearing into the hedges surrounding Angelito's patio. What he can't remember is if he wiped off his prints before throwing it away.

Invisibility, he prays in silence, but his wish is immediately annulled by the blinding flash of a camera.

TWO DEATHS FOR ÁNGELA

BY ANA MARÍA FUSTER LAVÍN

Plaza del Mercado

> *chewing aspersions*
> *and spitting on bodies until the soul is soiled*
> —Anjelamaría Dávila

The first time I saw someone die was also the first time she and I came face-to-face. Her eyes met mine, then she turned around. She walked away to the rhythm of salsa in Taberna Los Vázquez; her footsteps and the old musicians' cadence entranced me. In the distance, someone called her with a voice very similar to my own: "Mita, c'mon." There, for an instant, we saw each other. She opened the door to another mirror. I was certain I was no longer alone.

It was December 28, Innocent's Day, and that night I'd gone to the little plaza in Santurce to meet up with my friends Omar and Margarita, who were celebrating their honeymoon. They'd set me up with a blind date, which, as usual, was shit. The aforementioned Don Juan, named Beto—Bert in English, like the stupid Sesame Street character, of course, not like Beto, the gorgeous singer of La Ley—passed the time reading me high-minded poems: *If Borges did this, if Che Meléndez did that* . . . I recalled another poet, who looked like a pigeon filled and about to burst with Vaseline. They found that bastard dead in the Plaza las Américas parking lot. I laughed to myself. My friends thought my blind date was making me nervous.

The night continued with a long monologue about Beto's studies in comparative literature and languages. I spaced out, remembering my last ex, a professor of English at the university who constantly talked about himself and about his ex-wife who'd taken his apartment and lived there with another woman and three cats. Beto had the same tone of voice and the same smugness. The chatter of this date was just as insufferable. "And that's why I hate cats," he said. I went to order two drinks. I looked at the clock. We'd been talking for forty-five minutes. *Another guy who hates cats*, I thought. *He must've also been dumped for being an idiot.*

"Why do you hate cats?" I asked him when I got back. He started to tell me about the cats of Cortázar, some other writer. Of course, then he complained about his last girlfriend, how she slept with her cat and how the cat's hair on the bed disgusted him. I thought about taking my revenge against his idiocies. I also thought about Mita, who disappeared down the street to the rhythm of the pleneras.

My friends were sitting and kissing among the avocado trees on the little plaza, and I asked Beto for a triple shot of vodka on the rocks. He'd had a shot of B-52 and I'd had a whiskey on the rocks. Alcohol helps me move apathetically in the face of cretinism. He continued his monologue, culminating in another of his poems.

This was the vilest, most damned Innocent's Day in my whole life. As tends to occur, he began to get clingy, cheesy, cunning. I remembered what my mother once told me: there are some men who are just like a bottle of beer—from the neck up, there's absolutely nothing.

"I'm leaving," I said.

"I'll walk you."

"No, I live nearby down Canals, turn on Primavera, and keep going to Estrella, straight up to Bayola."

"Look, beautiful, it's dangerous for a woman to go that way alone, I'll walk you. Besides, the night can't just end so quickly."

I stared at him, waiting for him to comprehend that he was fucking up my night. What a cesspit of a man. "I'm leaving now," I told him.

"Don't be silly, it's still early. C'mon, Ángela, don't be mad." The poet moved closer, almost grazing his chest against mine, running his hand across my hip.

"I'm leaving."

"Don't be mad."

"I'm leaving."

"I'll walk you. Really, it can be dangerous."

"Let's go then, but be quiet and don't touch my ass."

I picked up my pace. We were passing under the graffiti-covered bridge, and in the distance I saw Mita disappearing into the shadows. I smiled. Beto was beside me, he stroked my back, resuming his monologue, and brought his hand down to grab mine. I felt the brush of his lips against my neck, like a poltergeist. I pulled away and shoved him. He fell down in the street and groaned. He was drunk, and when he tried to stand up, he slipped and fell again. Unfortunately for him, a car was passing by at full speed, and it hit him.

I hid around a corner at the end of the bridge. I'd heard the crunch of his bones, his moan mixed with the whisper of blood escaping his mouth. The driver had fled. My soul took flight too, escaping through my throat. I hurried to my apartment, assuming the worst, imagining his body crushed like a trampled dove. I was so scared that I thought I was dying as I tried to open the door to my apartment.

I poured myself a glass of wine and stayed in the little room with my computer. I looked at my hands, which shook, and drank, drank, and shook. I got a text from Margarita asking where I was. I replied that I'd escaped from Beto because he was a waste of time, that he'd gone to buy some drinks at Velázquez, and so I'd left. Margarita texted me that she thought she'd seen him talking to some friends of hers. Could he be alive? Impossible. I didn't tell her what'd happened, danger disappears if you ignore it. I wrote: *Don't set me up on any more blind dates.* She replied with a sad face and told me good night, the next time she'd find me someone more fun.

I kept drinking wine and writing. My hands, fallen into insomnia, kissed psychedelic shadows that wrapped themselves in the silence of the pathetic memories of that night, of old exes and future loves, until I fell asleep. I got an unexpected text, an ex who wanted to see me, he was drunk, no doubt. I dreamt again about the poet's blood, about Mita, and about a poem dancing in my bedroom.

* * *

I woke up at sunrise with the sensation that it all had been an illusion. I was confused. The whispers of loneliness suffocated me. I opened the door of my apartment and saw a dead dove. I closed it quickly and slid the little chain. Terror gripped my spine. I looked at my phone: no calls. I turned on the news: they weren't covering the poet's death. And yet, I expected that they'd come to arrest me any minute. I ate a light breakfast and wrote all day long, as well as the next day and the next, trying to free myself from my amputated memories.

I didn't leave my apartment until New Year's Eve. Mami had called to have me come over on New Year's with them. I went as far as the door, lay down to peek below it, saw nothing. My hands shook, I made it into the hallway. In the area in front of the building's entrance, some kids were playing with a ball, and Doña Cleo, the lottery ticket vendor, gave me a number for free. I went to a nearby supermarket that had a cafeteria, and I ordered rice with chicken, potato salad, and the newspaper. I texted Margarita and she replied that she was in New York with her cousins.

I took out my notebook so I could write while I ate, and I remembered the voice that'd called to Mita, so similar to mine, almost my own voice—the moment that I knew I wasn't alone. It isn't loneliness that suffocates me, but the recycling of pasts, the shadows of the witching hour, my Aunt Mabel reproaching me for not marrying or having kids, going to a party and right away someone asking about my ex, or why I don't have a boyfriend, or why I work in a bookstore when I could be a university professor. What's suffocating about loneliness is other people. For a few seconds I felt bad for Beto, but I rid myself of the feeling quickly. Some memories bring negative consequences. I kept writing.

I listened to my neighbor, girl of the eternal *dubi dubi*, who was protesting into her cell phone because she'd called the salon and they didn't have a single appointment available to dye her hair and fix her nails. "The biggest tragedy since Fortuño lost the governorship," she said. I couldn't write anymore. I got up, wanting to tell her what I really thought: *Who do you think you are? Do you think your life matters to anyone?* Instead, I went to buy some wine and cheese to take to Mami's house. In the hallway, I ran into the neighbor girl and muttered, "Cunt."

I went down Calle Loíza toward the intersection with San Beto. There was an AMA bus at the stoplight. I looked at the window. There was a girl there, reading; she lowered the book and looked at me with a slightly surprised smile. My reaction was the very same smile and a powerful attack of arrhythmia. The light turned green, the bus continued on its way, and I continued on mine toward San Beto. One by one, my footsteps sank into the memory of the woman in the window. She looked just like me, I was certain. I felt a little light-headed and sat down in the parking lot across from the synagogue. I lowered my head. I was sweating, a cold sweat. I opened my eyes and Mita was sitting beside me. I tried to touch her, but she moved quickly off toward a nearby Catholic school, and I headed on to the condo where Mami lived, just past the children's hospital.

That night I rang in the new year in Mami's apartment, with my three brothers, their wives, and my nieces and nephews; also Julio, a neighbor from Spain who was a cook at a pizzeria in Hato Rey. The kids watched YouTube videos on a tablet, my mom prepared rice and beans, and my brothers and sisters-in-law talked about their jobs, inescapable even on vacation. Their lives are as small as their offices, like worlds all their own where the rest of us are invisible.

Mami was sad because January 1 was the five-year anniversary of our father's death, and she cooked to forget. She runs a little business where she sells carrot and amaretto cakes at the bookstore on Ponce de León. Mami respects my individuality, so she doesn't ask questions about my life. She's also the only one who reads my childish stories. I told her that I thought I'd killed a boy. She laughed as if I'd delivered a Cantinflas monologue, and said, "You wouldn't even kill in your dreams." She gave me a kiss and poured two cups of coffee-flavored Pitorro.

Julio, also invisible to my brothers and their wives, was on the balcony. I poured him some of the Pitorro and we chatted for a while. He talked about new pizza recipes, about a Dominican lover he had three years ago who'd slather him with coconut oil before they made love. As we drank more, we reached a complicit silence. We looked out at the city from the balcony, and I told him about the woman I'd seen who was identical to me, that I thought I'd killed someone, and even about my two encounters with Mita. Julio told me that sometimes nightmares mix with memories and these memories are all we have left when everyone's abandoned us. We hugged and gave each other a light kiss on the lips. We'd always wanted each other, but never found the synchrony in our lives to be together. That's our destiny, we, the others.

Julio began to grow pale. He clenched his jaw, his eyes seemed to be popping out of their sockets. He pressed his chest and was sweating as if it were noon on a summer day. He grabbed my shirt and I started to scream for Mami and my brothers. Julio vomited on me, pissed himself, and collapsed to the floor. I tried to stand him up, I took his pulse, I gave him mouth-to-mouth. Nothing. At last, my brother Alberto came and helped me try to resuscitate him. My sister-in-law Teresa called 911. The ambulance arrived twenty minutes later. Julio died at my feet of a massive heart attack, in an ocean of vomit and piss.

It was very late when Mami was finally, after a few tranquilizers, able to fall asleep. I left silently. The street was deserted, the fog from the cool morning hung in the air, mixing with the smoke from all the fireworks that had roared, bidding farewell to an unforgettable year. It's nice to walk in the early morning. Those seconds spilled into the air incessantly, just empty games, spells armed with lies, like stopping the breath of a dead man to give last rites to another illusion.

Mita appeared in the dark alley that took me from Calle del Parque to Avenida de Diego. I told her that Julio had died before ringing in the new year. I cried a little. She looked at me. We continued on our way and a vagrant vomited on the curb. I caught him just as he was about to fall, and sat him down. He looked like a zombie; he fell asleep like that. I left him a container with a little bit of rice and beans, two pasteles, and a drumstick. Mita rubbed against my legs. She also was a creature of the night.

Another resident of the street slept on the sidewalk in the light of Pizzeria Macabre (the name that my ex had given it). There, three musicians played their last notes among Medallas and cigarettes. The flute player offered to buy me a drink. He told me that his home was the night and loneliness was his lover. The New Year's Eve celebrations intoxicated us with greater nostalgias than the alcohol. I said goodbye to him and took a couple bottles of beer in my backpack. Mita was waiting for me and we went on our way in silence. I was ready to invite her to come stay with me if she wanted. But after opening the condo door, I looked back and she was already gone.

I woke up after midday. I was weak; I had a coffee and sat down to write. I remembered that I might've killed a man, that these days death was caressing my footsteps. I also remembered the girl who looked like me. Seeing myself in the mirror of death or the mirror of another life, parallel to my own maybe. Just seeing myself confronting the possibility of being someone else.

Already nightfall, I got a text from Margarita telling me to be careful, not to go walking at night, that she'd had a nightmare in which I was attacked by a woman. At that moment, they knocked on my door. Two police officers. They asked me if I knew Beto Matías and Angelina Fabrani. I said I'd gone out with Beto one night in Santurce. They asked me where I'd been that night. I told them. They asked me if I was Angelina Fabrani. I said my name is Ángela, last name Fuentes. They asked me to accompany them to the precinct on Calle Hoare with my ID. There I learned that Beto and Angelina were suspected of beating a vagrant, a woman, and a cat that morning, and leaving them to die, bleeding out, dismembered. They showed me a photo and I started to cry. It looked like Mita and the vagrant to whom I'd given the food.

After four or five hours, they let me go. I called Mami on my way home. She was calm. I continued walking, with the feeling that I was being followed. I picked up my pace. I called Margarita. She didn't answer; neither did Omar. I sensed footsteps almost on my heels. A hand touched my shoulder. When I looked behind me, I saw myself. The other me laughed with a voice similar to mine, but it wasn't my laugh.

I pushed her and started to run, then looked back. There was no one. I ran down Ponce de León to Calle Canals. I continued to my building without stopping. At the pizzeria on the corner there were two patrol cars and an ambulance. I approached. There was a black shoe on the ground, a case on the other side. I picked it up; it contained my friend's flute. I went as close as the onlookers and police would allow.

The man's nose was broken, under his bare feet the blood formed a pool. His left eye was about to pop, a piece of his glasses stuck into it. He called to me and I went to him. I hugged him and cried. He said, "Be careful, my girl." He passed out, then they took me away from him and put him in the ambulance.

A hand blew me a kiss from a car that passed slowly by. I was sure that it was the other me; I heard her mocking laugh. I tried to run after her and I slipped. I stepped in the enormous pool of the flute player's blood and sank into an immense darkness. It smelled like death. When I opened my eyes, I was sitting in one of the booths in the pizzeria. One of the musicians, my violinist friend Javi, had bought me a vodka with orange juice. He smiled, with traces of bitterness in his expression, and said: "You fainted when you tried to wave to someone." We drank together, but almost without talking. I kissed the corner of his lips, and he hugged me tightly against his chest. We kissed softly, those kisses recovering something of our lost humanity, or the last hidden orgasm before dying. We said goodbye with a nod. He didn't get up.

Walking home, my footsteps sank into the asphalt. I lowered my eyes but couldn't see past my knees, my feet and legs were beneath the street. I got to the stairway with my waist almost touching the concrete. Mita was sitting in front of the door to my apartment. Her tongue flicked across the tip of my nose. At last I started to feel like I'd recovered my body. For a while I forgot the past hours, but not the smell of blood. Mita lay down on the sofa. I poured myself some wine and turned on the computer. I had to write to recover. I had the sensation of living different lives.

I returned to myself. My fingers fell between the moldering memories, between my thighs too; I was touching myself, I recognized my lips, my clitoris. I masturbated as I wrote, and my blood moaned metaphors. Maybe each word could rescue me, splitting apart every scar of my fears. The words and my body melted together, the living words, my hot cunt. I could feel that other me kissing my neck, her hands playing with my nipples; I got even more wet. I thought about how that other me had to be that Natalie, and about Mita, and about all the deaths too. The two of them were always nearby when they occurred. That other me, could it be possible? My pussy convulsed, my other hand wrote automatically on the keyboard. At last I could cry out.

In the morning my cell phone woke me. It was Javi, the violinist. He asked me how I was feeling and invited me to breakfast. He told me that the flute player had died shortly after arriving to the hospital. While we were talking, I saw Mita jump off the balcony. I lived on the first floor, but it was still dangerous. I dropped my cell phone, ran after her, but couldn't see her anymore. I went back to the phone and asked Javi if I could come over, because I was feeling really messed up. I got a text from Margarita saying I should call her as soon as possible. I ignored it.

I got to Javi's apartment in Ciudadela around two in the afternoon. We talked, drank vodka, and ate sushi. He played a piece from a Tchaikovski concerto. Really, before the flute player's death, we'd only said hi to each other, talked about random things, had a drink. Tragedy often unites loneliness and desire. And yet I was truly captivated by this man's sadness.

When he finished the piece, I applauded and got undressed. Even at fifty, his expression was still that of a boy with a Christmas present, a gift we gave each other in his bed. We made love tenderly, caressing each other slowly. Oral first, then I let him enter me, the coming and going of his body against mine, the squeak of the bedsprings, our sweat, and his hoarse moans when he came. I didn't have an orgasm, but I enjoyed it anyway.

"Do you think it's possible to have a double?" I asked him, naked on the bed, a postcoital purr.

"What are you talking about?"

"About how there's another version of you in the world, that you can cross paths with that identical person."

"I get it. I saw it in a movie."

"Last night I felt like I was making love with my double."

"That can be remedied, mine has found its second life."

He put my hand on his hard cock and kissed my neck. After getting wet, I climbed on top of him and tried to think of nothing, riding him hard until I finally had an orgasm and he came between my thighs. He told me softly: "Someday you're going to fall in love with me."

I was hypnotized, looking at a photo I saw on a shelf above his desk. It was Beto, but in Spanish military attire, and a woman with a familiar face. "Those are my parents," he managed to tell me when the intercom started buzzing. Javi answered it, then looked at me, frightened. "It's my ex-wife, we split up six months ago, she's furious because the divorce papers came. Please, go down the stairs in the hallway. Forgive me, I love you, I'll call you."

I said nothing. I got dressed quickly and went down the stairs. I heard them screaming at each other as I left Javi's building. I crossed over to Libros Ac and bought a graphic novel. Then I ordered a craft beer and sat down at a little table in front of the window. I saw clothes and some women's boots falling from Javi's balcony. I thought I heard a gunshot. Samuel, the bookseller, looked at me with surprise, I stared at him uncomprehendingly and said goodbye.

The seventh time I ran into Mita, it was a few blocks away from there. I was smoking a cigarette, Margarita didn't answer my calls, Mami neither. Just how you're sometimes surprised by your own stupidity, it occurred to me to call Javi. His wife answered and said, "Fucking whore! If I find out who you are, I'll shoot you too." I sat down right there on Calle Canals and cried inconsolably. Mita stayed close to me; she was nervous, as if wanting me to pay attention to her, for us to get out of there.

I looked up and I saw my other, Angelina, standing in front of me, handing me a handkerchief and a folded piece of paper. She turned around, and as she tried to cross Ponce de León, an AMA bus hit her; I heard the screech of the brakes already on top of her and the crunch of bones. When I stood up, there were two young men in front of me. One grabbed me, held a knife to my throat, and said in my ear, "You look prettier when you're quiet, bitch. If you move or scream, you die."

Meanwhile, the other one put his hands in my pockets, took out my cell phone, my wallet, my iPad mini, lowered my zipper, and stuck his hand in. "If I could, I'd eat your pussy right here, and nobody would notice." I kicked him in the face and his friend cut my throat, hard like a guillotine.

I watched them run down Canals. I fell slowly to the sidewalk; I saw the folded paper flying through the air. I saw her, me, dead, I saw myself dying. Mita licked my forehead, meowed, and I watched her disappear down Calle Canals, across Ponce de León, losing her around the old Telégrafo building. A blank page floated through the air, landing in front of my face. I already felt nothing.

MATCHMAKING

BY MAYRA SANTOS-FEBRES

Buen Consejo

They called him Koala because even while executing his victims, he did not appear totally awake. He had a swollen face and belly, and Koala Gutiérrez often spent hours chomping on a little twig, a "chewing stick," as it's known in Nigeria. He'd served there, first as a soldier, later as a sergeant in his government's peacekeeping forces. It wasn't exactly his government, but the government of the island. His island floated in the middle of the Caribbean. They speak Spanish there, but it's a territory of the US. And the army is operated by a government separate from but in control of his own, giving it an international presence on this planet. In other words, he left the island as a member of the peacekeeping forces of a country that occupies his own, with the goal of maintaining order in a country that had none. They hadn't declared war on his country nor on the country that wasn't his, but were internationally committed to maintaining a false peace. Or something like that.

All of that happened in the eighties. After serving, it was easy for Koala Gutiérrez to obtain more work as a mercenary soldier. He lived in Africa for ten years, fighting in various wars. The one in Sierra Leone was the last—he got sick of it and went back to his homeland.

Koala's homeland wasn't really the island. He only ever knew a slice of it before enlisting in the army when he was just eighteen. At that time, Koala was already an immensely fat kid who didn't mess with anybody and was lethal in a fight. A well-placed punch, a chokehold around the neck, and *boom*. No enemy was a match for Koala. And in Las Margaritas almost everyone was an enemy.

Koala was from Las Margaritas, an apartment project that the government (of his country? of the other country?) had built to provide shelter for the thousands of starving families living on the edge of Laguna San José. His was like all the other apartments: a square box made of concrete, with one bathroom, two bedrooms, and bars in all windows, where a family of six had to live. His parents were like many other parents, shadows of hunger and rage, who'd left the countryside and come to the city to look for work, finding it occasionally. One afternoon Koala's father got lost in the labyrinths of little streets, pastures, and trash dumps that surrounded Las Margaritas, and never came back. His mother told him he went north, to that other country. To help out, his mother brought his grandmother from the country to live with them.

Koala could spend incalculable hours sleeping. He ate, slept, and chewed on his little stick—or on a leaf or a plastic straw, anything he could shove in his mouth—and then he'd sleep some more. He was never good in school. He never showed any interest in anything that didn't require the absolute minimum effort. And in fights. He never initiated any, but he won them all. So when he was old enough, he enlisted in the army. And afterward, he came back. He never had children, no regular lover, not even an irregular one. He never got into sleeping with ex-convicts, the ones who got out of prison and came back to Las Margaritas, after years spent surrounded by men, a new need in their bodies. Not with the sad little whores who sold themselves on the project streets for drugs, either. "This guy only uses what he's got between his legs to piss," heckled Chino, a distant cousin, who got him into the business and introduced him to the Boss. "Just like a koala bear. Hanging from his pole all day, snoring away without a care." Koala stayed silent and stared at him with his dark, round eyes.

But now he had to keep those eyes open. He was sitting next to Ballpoint in Café Violeta, waiting for his next victim: a woman. "La Pastora" had moved through the ranks and turned into a solid rival for the Boss in the interminable battle for domination of the drug trade. She had inherited control from her dead brother, and inexplicably emerged as a lethal power, a force from which it was necessary to be protected. That's why the Boss contacted Koala. "Go with Ballpoint, he knows her movements. Get her out of my way. Nothing fancy, maybe a quick shot in the forehead." He didn't know why the Boss qualified it. That was Koala's classic method. A shot to the head, infallible, between the eyebrows. No bloody mess. No bodies full of holes. Clean and wholesome, Koala guaranteed a tranquil death, and he was famous for not even giving his victims time to scream.

But he didn't like killing women. He'd seen too many ruptured bellies in the war. Too many women raped by militia soldiers and then hacked up by machetes, bodies rotting in the savannah. Exposed flesh, just before exploding, had the consistency of plastic. The butchery of a woman's body turned his stomach more than anything.

When the Boss informed him about La Pastora, he thought about saying no. He was about to shake his head when something stopped him. What woman could be a boss in the drug trade? In other words, does she really count as a woman if she's gotten her hands dirty—not with blood, which is easy (Koala knows it), but with terror transformed into blood in the eyes of her enemies? How many addict children—now corpses, because of some stupid drug debt—had she, personally, turned over to their mothers? Koala imagined La Pastora as a brutish woman, shapeless, with short hair and swollen hands. A broad back just like his. Or like a frigid whore, one of those skinny, painted women with plastic everything, who so many people like and who leave him wanting to stay eternally asleep.

"I work alone," he responded to the Boss.

"I want you to take Ballpoint. He'll point her out. The thing is, it has to be her."

He never could've imagined what he saw: a woman soft as velvet entered Café Violeta; she was full-figured, with a mature head of hair that smelled like cinnamon and eucalyptus—long, straight, and a little stiff, like a mane. All of her was brown, or really the color of honey. She half-closed her small, round eyes with the lust of someone who had just awakened from a long dream. Koala intuited that her very large breasts had dark nipples, enough in them to suckle for all eternity. Her thighs pressed against each other under her skirt, which fell to the middle of her calf—they were the thighs of a woman who'd known children. Firm hips, wide rump. Koala had to close his eyes after watching her pass by. He smelled her walk down Café Violeta's central hallway; he heard her sit down at a table in the back. Three men stationed themselves around La Pastora, three men similar to him who were obviously her bodyguards.

"That's her," Ballpoint whispered in his ear, and left.

With eyes wide open, Koala Gutiérrez kept watch. He was also watching inside. Flesh, touch, an erection. The aroma of eucalyptus and cinnamon made him alert. He saw how La Pastora ordered a coffee with milk; how the owner of the place sat down to chat with her for a while; how she finished conversing with the owner of Café Violeta at the same time that she finished her coffee. His prey would soon be making a change of scene. Koala Gutiérrez asked for his bill and paid it, chewing on his stick. He'd wait for them in the car.

La Pastora left Café Violeta five minutes later. She and one of her henchmen got into a new SUV, subtle gold, like her. Koala prepared to follow her, his eyes lit up like two sparks in the night.

They turned down Avenida Borinquen and took the road down to the boat launches. They crossed a new bridge heading toward Las Margaritas, turned around at the roundabout at San Juan Bosco Church, and entered the ramp that connected to the housing project. Koala followed them in silence. Suddenly, his sixth sense tingled. Along that route, most of the roads were closed down for repairs from the recent rains, when the laguna flooded the banks of Las Margaritas. Koala stepped on the accelerator.

It smelled like a trap.

He couldn't explain where the car that hit his vehicle on the driver's side came from. Koala lost control and struck a lightpost in a flat area near the entrance to Las Margaritas. The owner's manual for the vehicle pressed against his chest. He felt like he was suffocating, but then two hands pulled him out.

La Pastora was waiting for him. A single look and Koala Gutiérrez knew he'd never be able to shoot this woman in the head. He'd never be able to shoot her, period. He'd rather kiss her.

The bodyguards held him by his hands and feet. Koala put up no resistance; he didn't get desperate.

He closed his eyes and imagined himself caressing that woman's long hair, sinking his massive, clumsy hands into that flesh dressed in leaves and spices. He imagined La Pastora looking at him in the same way, savoring him. But in his imagination, he caught sight of a strange light in her gaze. It was a cold light, like that of a deranged animal. He wanted to look away. He kept imagining how his hands would slide along her soft belly; how he'd push them down to find the mound between her legs. Then he saw himself bending over and lifting La Pastora's skirt, burying his face between her thick legs, licking them, opening them. Koala bit La

Pastora, chewed on her slowly, drank her down in an instant, and for all eternity. At last, he opened his eyes.

"You can kill me now," he said.

Two shots sounded.

PART II

CRAZY LOVE

DOG KILLER

by Luis Negrón

Trastalleres

C haro gives me a strange look when I tell her I'll be right back. "It's Monday," she says.

We never go out on Mondays. Sometimes Tuesday comes and we don't go out either.

"I'll be back quick, baby."

I'm wearing shorts and sandals so she doesn't say anything. Charo doesn't look at me. She looks at the telenovela. I'm about to say something, but she grabs the remote and turns up the volume.

Outside there is no one to be seen. All the streetlights are broken. I stop at the corner and see the light in the guardhouse at La Corona, two blocks down. That guy never comes out, not even when he hears gunshots. Three times people have gone in to rob the place and he stays inside. Later, he says he didn't see anything or anyone. I don't blame him.

Last night I left the bag near Bomberos, in an empty lot where Matatán says there used to be a racetrack for horses, but they demolished it. What Matatán doesn't know he invents. Charo calls him Wikipedia. I enter as if to take a piss and I grab the bag. The bitch is heavy. I'm afraid it will drip blood, but I throw it over my shoulders. I hope it doesn't move.

Last night I dreamed about that fucking dog. I was little, and Mami was hanging up clothes behind a house that wasn't our actual house, but in the dream it seemed to be. At some point, Mami lets out a shout and speaks to me in English, and I don't understand but I answer her in English too, and she says: *Look.* When I look, Lazaro's dog is above the septic tank and he's big, the fucker. Like a house. Mami tries to cover him with a sheet that she's hanging out, but the dog dodges, and she throws it over me without meaning to. *It's me, Mami,* I say. And I feel the dog on top of me, and Mami stops talking, but I don't remove the sheet so that the dog won't see me—so I won't see.

Charo hadn't shown up. Ever since she came up with the Ecuador thing, she's been spending more time on the street. Sometimes at 15th, in front of Levy's, sometimes at Fernández Juncos. At eight she was already there. If I dropped by while making the rounds, she lost her shit.

"What?" she'd say. "What's up?"

I'd say nothing and leave. The cars don't stop if they see me. She's going to kill herself. She's going to fuck herself over.

I turned on the TV so I'd forget the dream. I was pissing myself but was afraid to get up. Fucking dog, fucking Lázaro. I told myself that it'd be better to come clean to Charo. *Look, Charo,* I thought, *listen to me, I was the one who took out your brother,* the fucker. He had it coming. Because of the thing with Landi. But I knew better. Every time Lázaro did something, or stopped paying, or let something slip, and I told her about it, Charo would say: "My brother is sick. Only a piece of shit messes with a junkie."

That's what she called him, *My brother.*

But Landi had given him too many chances. When he found out about the most recent thing, he didn't say anything. Charo went to square things with him, but he said, "Forget it." I knew what was coming, but I didn't think he'd send me.

"Your turn," Landi said to me.

Shit, shit, I thought. *Fucking shit.* I shit on Lázaro's mother, that fucker. I tried to say something to Landi, but he looked at me the way he looks at you when he's had it up to here and it's better to just shut up.

That was last Wednesday.

It was easy to find Lázaro. I saw the dog on the corner first, on Calle Las Palmas. Mami always said that dogs smell fear. *If you're passing by a stray, don't get scared because they'll know and that's when they bite.*

"Cuñi, come here," I said to Lázaro. "Get in, Charo wants to see you, she's about to leave for Ecuador. Come find her with me, she wants to say goodbye to you. Get in."

"Give me something first, I'm jonesing, pai."

I had brought what Landi had given me and a Whopper. So he'd be happy.

"I'll be right there," he said.

"Here, here," I said to the dog, giving it the Whopper. Lázaro went behind the aqueduct so I wouldn't see him doing his thing.

Right away, the dog sunk its teeth into the hamburger and fries. It raised its head and stared at me, like it knew something.

Charo said her brother was respectful. That he never fixed in front of anybody. Whenever he came home he wore long sleeves, for the marks.

"He's good like that, always so humble." But the thing with Papi fucked him up. She never told me what the thing with Papi was. I asked her once and she just shrugged. Charo looked like a real woman, but people made fun of her shoulders. I didn't like it when she wore a tube top to come out with me. People looked at us. They looked at her, because of her shoulders.

Lázaro wanted to put the dog in the truck and I said, "No way, loco. Just no."

"But they'll take him. And besides, what's the big deal? This truck is a junker."

"Who the hell is going to take that bag of bones?" I asked, signaling with my hand for him to get in right away.

"The city people, Cuñi. Or someone."

I said no dog, and told him to hurry up, that Charo was waiting, that we had to go find her on the docks. That she was with the trick from Puertos. He got in and kept looking back to where the dog was until we turned the corner.

"He'll wait for me. One time, when Charo put me in a program, he waited a month for me. Since I give him food and stuff."

I didn't say anything.

"Ecuador . . . that's down farther. Down below Colombia. Is that where Lake Titicaca is? . . . I'm happy for her, man. God willing, everything will come out fine. Get her out of all this, loco. Once she has the operation you won't need to stay. Hey, that stuff you gave me is good," he said, leaning back in the seat.

He looked out the window. He had something of Charo, that mania she had for biting her lips when she smiled, of moving her knees when she sat down, nervously. They never looked anyone in the eyes; he looked down and she looked every which way.

Something smelled bad. I didn't know if it was him, the dump, or the mangrove. The Kennedy always stinks. His hands looked like gloves full of water.

I regreted that it was such a short drive. We entered the same dock as always. I'd been there many times, doing things for Landi. I turned off the lights.

When I got to Landi's place, they were setting up one of those bouncy houses for neighborhood kids. When he saw me he said something to Domi, who ran off and grabbed something from the freezer. He came up to me, but I didn't want to take the payment. I didn't say anything, I just gestured to Landi, as if to say that I'd see him later, and he understood.

I was going to go to Ponce de León to check on Charo, but I thought I'd better not. I headed home, went up on the roof. I smoked. I could see the docks from there. I closed my eyes, hard. Very hard.

Charo spent the money for the ticket to Ecuador on the funeral. Not the money for the operation. She didn't say much during those days. She didn't even go out on

Thursday, which is her best night. Finally, on Friday, she got dressed and was about to leave.

"Stay," I told her. "I'll cover your ticket. You know—"

"I'll pay for my cunt myself," she said, and she didn't say anything else.

The cable company had cut the building's stolen connections, and all we got was channel six. It was showing a black-and-white movie and I sat down to watch it. It was Santurce a long-ass time ago. I knew because of the Metro Cinema and the Labra School. The Ponce de León was full of people, many wearing hats. And that's when I heard the bark. I thought it was the TV, but no. Another bark. I looked out. It was Lázaro's dog. Furious.

That fucking dog, what does he want? I thought.

It wasn't barking at my building. I thought it was a cat or something, but then I saw it was barking at my truck, which I'd parked out front. It went up and sniffed it. And it barked again.

"Shit, shit, shit. Fucker, get out of here, fucker," I said in a low voice, as if the dog could hear me.

If I go out there, it's going to come bite me, the mother-fucker. But if Charo comes and sees it barking at my truck, she'll know something. I went in and turned off the TV so I could think. *Shit. If I club it, it's going to squeal and people will tell Charo.* I went to look for a broom or something to use. There was no other way. I could kill it with one stone if I threw it hard enough. Papi had killed a dog once with a pick because it pissed on his car tires, and it didn't squeal. Mami had covered my eyes and ears.

Damnit, I said to myself, *fucking shit.*

Then something occurred to me. I went to the freezer,

pulled out a piece of meat, and grabbed the bat from the back door. I went out. I looked around and there was nobody. The bulbs in the streetlights were still fucked. The dog saw me and went quiet. It lowered its head. Its problem wasn't with me. It looked at me, it looked at the meat in my hand, it looked at the truck.

Once, when we had cable, Charo and I watched a competition of people who looked like their dogs on Don Francisco. Charo, dying of laughter, said: "If my brother went on with his dog, he'd win. They're the same. And look, they're giving a thousand bucks. Overdose."

It did look like Lázaro, in how its eyes and head were always down. In how skinny it was, how black. I stretched out my hand and showed it the meat. It thought about it for a second, but eventually went over. I let it eat until it was done, and *boom*.

The bag weighed more than I remembered. Clearly it had died very satisfied, the fucker. Like Lázaro.

SAINT MICHAEL'S SWORD

BY WILFREDO J. BURGOS MATOS

Río Piedras

> *Blessed Michael, Archangel,*
> *defend us in the hour of conflict;*
> *be our safeguard against the wickedness*
> *and snares of the devil*
> —From the prayer to Archangel Saint Michael

> *At that time Michael, the great prince who*
> *stands guard over the sons of your people, will arise.*
> —Daniel 12:1

> *Yo voy a pedir, oye, por usted.*
> *Yo voy a pedir por todo a mi San Miguel.*
> —Evaristo Fama

Ángel knew that as soon as he turned away from the light at the end of the tunnel, pain awaited him on the other side of Avenida Gándara. If it hadn't been for the forceful whisper of his favorite song, floating to his ear from the cantina on the corner, he never would have awoken from what he thought was his voyage to eternity. Ramiro, to whom he'd sworn his love two months earlier, was the last image he remembered when he opened his eyes around noon on Friday. There was no clear indication as to how he got there, and he was almost bleeding out, his right side shot through with a bullet from an AK-47. Panicked, he hobbled toward the house of his sister Mariela, who was a nurse, to get fixed up and to find the culprit.

"Mari, open up, please. Open the fucking door," he moaned from the depths of his intestines.

"I'm coming, let me change the baby," she answered calmly.

"Hurry up, I'm dying!"

Mariela came outside, desperation spilling from her eyes. She knew Ramiro was involved.

"I told you to stop seeing that guy, that nothing good would come of it. Look how he just left you for dead. Wait till I get my hands on him," she rambled furiously, unable to stop talking even to catch her breath.

Ángel just looked at her and attempted to stay alert, but he was very tired. Bleeding, he'd already walked halfway across Río Piedras to arrive at the García Ubarri housing project. Yet he was also full of anticipation. He knew he'd be able to get revenge for the attempted murder, but he needed to find the perpetrator and Ramiro— he had to know something. There was an unease hiding behind the cover of night that was settling over San Juan, producing a sinister halo from the streetlights over the pavement. It gave him peace knowing that the darkness would hide his next moves until he was able to settle the score. Ángel wanted to take justice into his own hands.

* * *

A few hours later, after resting and drinking a chamomile tea, he left, even as Mariela implored him to spend the night. He barely heard her, the tingling along his spine gnawing at his conscience. He wanted to silence the agonizing hum assaulting his ears. Evil voices whispered to him from distant depths. With rage in every pore and experiencing vengeful pangs of melancholy, he followed his instincts.

He crossed the street in front of his sister's house and headed south down Calle Georgetti until he came to the corner of Avenida Ponce de León. There he ran into Lutgardo, the greatest diva ever born in the Caribbean. If it weren't for his ten-dollar blow job specials, Lutgardo's daughter Roberta would be eating dirt and water with chikungunya-carrying mosquitoes for breakfast, lunch, and dinner. Thank God there was something in the school cafeterias for his offspring. Lutgardo, who had lost his wife at just the right time to freely and fiercely suck each and every cock that crossed his path, had been liberated, literally, by the death of the greatest dumbass in America. His wife had tolerated his nocturnal outings and taken the money for the girl they had procreated.

"Hija de puta, how the fuck are you even here? You're gonna make me faint! Who gave you mouth-to-mouth? Did you know that Alejandro sucked you off while you were bleeding to death? It all happened so fast that the police just left you lying there, to see who'd feel bad for you!" Lutgardo yelled like a bitch in heat.

"Lower your voice, coño, you're always such a loud-mouth. I just left my sister's house, she fixed me up. Do you know what happened last night? I wanna know who had the balls to do this to me. What've you heard from Ramiro?" Ángel was worried.

"Ay, I don't know, they picked all of us up sucking Condado cocks. The raid was bullshit, mamita. I just ran out of there, screaming, protecting myself. You know not even Pope Francis is going to get my hard-earned money, baby. I only found out what I told you about Alejandro because Felicia told me. Ramiro got out of there early and you'd gone off, I don't know where," the diva rattled off as the bus that would take him home pulled up.

After an over-the-top, marvelously vivid, but quick goodbye from Lutgardo, Ángel went about his business. He was starting to grow impatient, so he got ready to go down to Calle Manila to find Felicia, whatever it took. Drops of blood slipped down his sides and rippling lower back muscles that made his butt the ideal preamble—an ass so juicy and perfect it satisfied even the most depressed. He thought about how he'd been sucked off by more than a hundred men before becoming enthralled with Ramiro. Ángel took a breath and let his tongue— the ruin of so many—hang out, revealing a weariness that only a cold beer would alleviate, the pain from his wound making his hands and knees tremble. He had a moment to pause before going to pester Felicia with questions, but all he had in his pockets was a slippery, sticky grape condom, used and broken. "The truth is, I'm a major leaguer," he muttered to himself while searching for the nearest trash can. In light of his empty pockets, he'd have to haggle for a drink to calm his thirst. He arrived at the bar La Solución and greeted his friends who, choking back tears, offered him everything, even the hand of the owner's granddaughter. Ángel could still pick up any girl he wanted with his dashing looks and strapping body. If his friends ever found out how many men he'd blown and that the rumors were true, at the very least they'd revive the Holy Inquisition in America. Think how great it'd be to light the bonfire and witness the death of one of the most experienced cocksuckers in the metropolitan area. "Sentenced to death for being a faggot." Really, they should sentence him to death for "having sucked more cock than twice the population of Puerto Rico." But there he was, más macho que los machos, letting them tease and pamper him.

One, two, three, four, five, six bottles of beer coursed through his system and negated the presence of the acetaminophen. He no longer felt his wound—the alcohol was the perfect anesthesia for the difficult task of finding his assailant. When he knew that it was time to leave, he got up from the milk carton they'd given him to rest on and went out to meet his fate.

He knew that at first Felicia would be scared to death, and then she'd lose her shit when she picked up the holy stench of booze. He was never spared the sermon from his most conservative and Pentecostal of friends, even when she was overjoyed to find out that he was still alive.

"Prieta chula, what're you dooooing? Please, c'mon, come out here. I'm fabulous, feeling tip-top," he managed to slur drunkenly before a shriek of joy rang out from inside the house.

"Son of the Holy Mother, I can't believe you're here!" she said, crying with excitement. "Christ, forgive me, like a thief in the night you'll come to punish me for this dirty mouth, but I'd already imagined the worst. Ivette came to me with the story of how Alejandro sucked you off when you were on your deathbed, and I couldn't do anything, I was stuck here taking care of mami. But just wait till I see him—and Luis too, who supposedly you drove wild last night. I can't help imagining Ramiro's face."

Apparently, there wouldn't be a sermon that day. She invited him in and told him, in excessive detail, what'd been said. That everyone screamed and jumped, that what she knew about Ramiro was what was known about Rolandito (the little boy who was kidnapped in 1999, and never found), that the police enjoyed seeing all of them suffer. But unfortunately she didn't have the slightest idea what had happened prior to whatever incident had left part of his body mutilated.

Both of them were very upset and looking for explanations, and after she'd gone to get him a cup of freshly brewed coffee, a rumbling from the bowels of the earth made every corner of every room and every glass in the house tremble. It was an earthquake! The night occupied itself with swallowing the goodwill of the world. It consumed them, slowly, as if envying the plenitude of optimistic souls. The night made itself owner and mistress of every street, every tectonic movement. Blackout. Ángel and Felicia took each other by the hands and ran outside to find fat Saturnino, of the vice police, lighting a cigarette.

"Maricón, what're you doing here? I had you for dead. Alejandro's blow job revive you? I imagine that little mouth would suck anyone out of eternal rest."

"Ay, Saturnino, please, the last thing I need is your shit. What're you doing here? Did you feel the earthquake?" Ángel said.

"Big deal, papito! I've felt so much shaking in these ass cheeks that Mother Earth's fury disappears somewhere between balls, ass, tongue, and gut."

"Do you know what happened to me yesterday? Coño, you have to know," Ángel asked desperately, thinking that Saturnino, protector of the state, would be able to solve the mystery for him.

"Tres carajos. I wasn't on duty and these raids come out of nowhere like that. I know Ivette was around there, squeezing information outta everybody. Call her and ask because I've got to continue my rounds to see how many bitter old ladies have shit themselves, or how many crazy putas got scared by the earthquake."

Before Saturnino could escape, Ángel asked him, as a favor, to accompany him to the house of the boss woman from the barrio where they grew up. The moment had come to confront Ivette face-to-face, with her black flesh, soft and swollen tits, purplish mouth, and olive-green eyes. It was a moment to invoke the saints—the moment he would let himself be seduced by the great witch of Río Piedras.

Ivette had been a feared woman for multiple generations. Since the time of her great-great-grandparents, the smells of patchouli, cinnamon incense, and squash purchased in Plaza del Mercado were always present in the concrete space made of seashells. Ivette only spoke to three people: Felicia, Saturnino, and Ángel. The three pendejos were already assembled.

"You scared you'll get your ass chewed out over there?" Saturnino responded immediately.

Just then they heard screeches of joy because the lights were coming back on.

"That's not it. You know we can figure out what happened if we put together what the three of us know and heard. Coño, say yes and I promise to give you the blow job of your life. The greatest blow job in the universe . . . okay?"

"You promise to swallow?"

"No deal without that," Ángel said with the sly wink he used to ensnare Ramiro—of whom he still had no news.

The three of them got into the police car and drove across Santa Rita along the back streets, through the center of the town, until they came to the community of Capetillo. A yellow house with a white door that had sticks of incense tied to it was waiting for them. The enviable mistress of the house observed them through the window in her small consultation room. With a sweet and cunning voice, she invited them in.

"Do you want anything, mis amores? Give me a hug, bello. I watched you go far and look now how the roads of life have brought you back here. Do you need help?"

"What happened, Ivette? You're our last hope for figuring it out."

"I just saw when Alejandro climbed on top of you to suck you off. It seemed like your dick was just the antidepressant he needed," she explained calmly. "If you'd seen how precious the image was, you wouldn't be mad at him. But other than that, I don't know anything. Santurnino wasn't there, Felicia had stopped reading to us from the Bible earlier, well before everything went down, and Ramiro took off the moment you were left lying on the pavement."

Ángel had lost hope and wanted to give up. A faggot who got shot and was searching for the truth—it wasn't even worthy of the front pages of the papers. This was the plight of sex workers. So much whoring that as a consolation prize a desperate diva sucked your cock while you were sprawled on the pavement, in a spot where gum-chewing twelve-year-old girls walked by, cackling with their little boyfriends. To top it off, the horrifying fellatio was the only thing he knew for sure. Nobody was even certain how many had been picked up in the raid. Life, like always, was shoving Ángel's wounded face right into a shit-stained ass.

A few seconds later, a transformed yet still provocative Ivette took to her prized room of spirits. It was time to give him a reading.

"Mi vida, I see here that you are being stalked by a close love. I see that he's sad, I see tears. Do you know who I'm talking about?" Ángel stayed silent. "Ay, papito, ay, ay, ay . . . they wanna see you dead."

"Who? Please, tell me who!"

"Of that I cannot be sure—lemme see the cup. Nope. But you must protect yourself, you have to keep Saint Michael's sword with you at all times."

Ángel watched in silence as Ivette removed a little

gold sword from a drawer, which she quickly proceeded to bathe in a red liquid.

"With Saint Michael before you, Saint Michael beside you, Saint Michael behind you. Free this being from his enemies, Lord, and through Your esteemed prince, grant him his request. Amen." Ivette crossed herself. Still in a trance, she handed him the amulet.

As soon as the promiscuous vagabond held it, the mini-weapon shone even brighter. A terrible tightness in his wrists and a knot in every vertebra immobilized his body. The entire night he had longed to be rid of the darkness that'd inhabited his heart and the side of his body where the bullet passed through. For the first time since he had woken up on the pavement, he felt invincible.

"You've got to go to El Cajón de Madera, the answer is there," Ivette said before coming back to earth.

The place she was referring to was the central gathering point for all the whores in Puerto Rico. It'd already become a famous international landmark for the sex trade community. El Cajón de Madera transformed, every night, into a space of freedom that for so long had only been a chimera; it reflected the acceptance of diversity: an ode to excess that didn't judge any being on the earth. And there, every Thursday night, the same night that Ángel was shot, the disputes congealed along the age-old political lines. But at this time, Friday poking its head into the wee hours of Saturday morning, the den of sin transformed into a locus of desperation for those who hadn't picked up a client to at least pay for their daily meal at the local fast-food joint. In a very strange way, Fridays were the Great Depression of lust, of wanting to unzip your fly to give or receive favors from horny caribeñas. Ángel would follow the instructions.

When he came out of the room, Saturnino was half-asleep and Felicia was praying and reading Bible verses on her cell phone. His announcement left them stunned.

"Why go to El Cajón? That woman is crazy. The Lord will settle the score!" Felicia yelled.

"Doesn't matter to me. I've got to finish my round either way. My shift is almost over," said the fat cop, who'd drooled a little when he'd been dozing.

As he went down the stairs of Ivette's house, Ángel looked back at his spiritual guide, whose skin had suddenly been transformed into a dark shade that would terrify anyone. But he continued on his way, following behind his gossiping, meddlesome companions. If something stuck in Saturnino's and Felicia's heads, the next day it became the big news that everyone, even the walls, would know. Morbid tidbits nourished the peace that they'd lost long ago. Saturnino had nothing to do but try to escape from his job and be unfaithful to his old wife, who had spiderwebs for a cunt. As for Felicia, praying for indomitable whores used up more energy than fifteen anal penetrations. Nothing would stop them now. The attempted murder had produced a fertile mystery to be solved.

And so, with the gossip streak activated, the three pendejos of the night from Río Piedras made their triumphal entrance into the brothel, which reeked of an iron-y menstrual odor and old rum.

The stench of whores, thought Ángel. Without warning, he threw himself onto the nearly naked body of Luis—who gasped at seeing him alive, wagging his tail, thirsty for vengeance, hungry with questions. "Where's Ramiro? Tell me what happened last night," he asked his victim irreverently.

Luis silently pulled Ángel by the arm to one of the seven dark rooms that set the place apart from the capital city's other offerings. When the door closed behind them, they came together in a single mouth and began bumping into contours and walls varnished with remnants of beer and, who knows, possibly herpes. They held their heads up like they were swimming without knowing how to swim. They tried to look each other in the eye in the darkness and were left submerged in silence. They stroked each other's chests, backs, necks, and faces, confining themselves to the exodus of their bodies, ignoring the question of who'd shot whom. Both of them gave without malice, licked without reason, sucked without restraint. In the background, salsa music exuded sweat, the call-and-response ensnared them. They had reached fullness, a kind of nirvana in the din of the tropics.

Then, slowly, the music stopped like an afternoon jealously bidding farewell as it confronted the night. That evening, Ángel was unfaithful to the code of vengeance. The final notes of salsa touched what was left of each body. Bitterness made of barley, cigarettes, and cocaine sharpened every taste bud. Ángel felt Saint Michel's sword in his right pocket and he held back, just at the point of coming between Luis's thighs.

"Before I finish . . . What happened last night? I can't wait. Please tell me!" he yelled excitedly.

"Last night you ceased to exist."

Angry with himself, regretful, Ángel pulled away from the arms of his lover and ran out of the darkness toward the bathroom. There, he turned on the light, splashed his face, and stood in front of the full-body mirror. He realized then that there was nothing left of him but bloody tatters of skin, sparse hair, and a skin tone reflecting an anguish that cannot be explained—even by comparing it to the darkness of the street that had made him who he was: Ángel, of whom not even a scrap remained.

Devastated, with tears tracing the contours of his gaunt face, and tightly gripping the sword that would rid his life of all evil, he went back to the main dance floor where he'd left Saturnino and Felicia, but nobody was there. The place had become the somber desert of his unrealized dreams. After searching everywhere, he came to the end of the hallway of dark rooms, where he found himself face-to-face with the silhouette of Ramiro, who was pointing an AK-47 at him.

All of a sudden, he remembered that there was an exit behind the bar where he had escaped before when he got in trouble. Then, with only three long strides separating him from escape, he was deafened by an explosion as he opened the door to salvation and stumbled into a coffin—three red candles, a bouquet of roses, a cross, and a crowd who wept in remembrance while praying over his dead body.

A KILLER AMONG US

BY MANUEL A. MELÉNDEZ

Hato Rey Norte

I was up when Papi arrived. It was late—I'm sure it was past midnight—and I was still wide awake from all the thunder and lightning that had ransacked the small town of Hato Rey Norte.

I could tell Papi was drunk (which happened frequently) by his loudness and cursing. On the other hand, there was calmness in Mami's voice—like soft music to soothe the beast. It worked for a while, but as soon as he became quiet (just like the fading thunder overhead), he exploded again. I don't know whose rage was stronger—the storm's or my father's.

Despite all the turmoil, I eventually found sleep.

The early morning came in through my window, but not before my late grandfather's old rooster's annoying crowing. He was an ill-tempered creature that seemed to live for three reasons: to scream out his hoarse shriek, to harass the hens, and to stand guard by a hole in the back of the house where a nest of rats made their home.

Like a sentinel, the rooster would wait for them. The second an unsuspecting rat climbed out of the hole, the rooster would peck at it with precise deadliness. One day, forced by boredom, I sat on a rock and witnessed the old feathered bully kill two rats and send a third scurrying back into the hole, with both of its eyes pecked out of their sockets.

Grandpa always said that this particular rooster was no ordinary bird—it had a cursed spirit trapped inside its body. I knew grandpa was lying about the spirit, but there were times when the rooster would look at me with its beady eyes and I had to wonder if Grandpa was right after all.

Mami was sipping her coffee slowly in the kitchen when I came out of my room to go to school one morning. There was a distant look in her eyes, and it troubled me to see her like that. Her hair was brushed to one side, and even though she attempted to hide it, I could see the bruises on her face.

When she noticed me staring, she shifted her body and tilted her face. It was too late. All I could think at that moment was that I hated my father so much.

I knew that Papi had left for the sugarcane fields because I saw the empty hook next to the door where he hung his machete. The machete was his tool, and there were times when I felt like he treated that blade of steel better and gentler than he treated us. I relaxed when I saw its absence.

I went to the table where my mom sat and grabbed a piece of pan de manteca. Not bothering to plaster it with butter, like I always did, I took a big bite and spilled crumbs all over my shirt. "Bendición," I said to Mami, and without waiting for her blessing, I gathered my books and ran out.

The merciless sun had baked the dirt path. Most of the rain from the night before had dried, although a few little puddles remained. I reached the house that everyone in town called "La Casa Blanca"—because of its rotting walls and peeling white paint—and saw that my friend Carlito was waiting for me.

The house was an eyesore (not that we lived in luxury), a dump. It sagged low to the ground on one side, and the rusted zinc roof was ready to be ripped off by the next hurricane and sent straight to the ocean.

An old woman and her mentally ill daughter lived there. The daughter was in her thirties. She walked with a limp and always drooled, parading around the house naked. Drool and all, we took turns peeking at her unclothed body—salivating at her big brown nipples and what Carlito called "el gran ratón peluo" between her legs.

A truck weighed down by a load of sugarcane came wobbling up the hill at the bend in the road. There was an army of boys running after it, grabbing at the stalks and pulling them off. They hid the stalks at the side of the road and would pick them up later, at the end of the school day.

One of those boys was Guillermo—our fearless leader. He was one year older than we were and had been left back in the first grade. That extra year gave him superiority over me and Carlito, so we caught up to him and took our share of sugarcane.

I snapped a small piece off and began chewing on it after we'd hidden our prizes under a line of bushes not far from La Casa Blanca. We continued on our trek to school and the yellow school bus rumbled past us. We seldom took the bus, for we felt that only little kids and sissies rode it. We often imagined we were three soldiers returning home from war after killing the enemy.

It was the 1960s, after all, and imagination was a big thing.

Ahead of us was a small crowd gathered by an abandoned gas station—mostly housewives returning after dropping their kids off at school and old men too fragile to work the sugarcane fields. They were in the midst of a very serious conversation.

I couldn't hear what they were saying at first, but when we got closer I heard someone say, "Mataron a un hombre"—a man had been murdered.

Guillermo turned to us, and I knew by the look in his eyes that we would be taking a slight detour on our way to school. We lingered close enough to the group to listen, but not close enough for them to shoo us away.

"Did someone go to the police?" one of the wives asked, her hair still in rollers, dressed in a bata—a faded housedress.

A man next to her, his brown face carved with deep wrinkles, stared at her and spat on the ground. "What for? They can't do anything about it, he's already dead!"

"¿Pero qué van a hacer? You can't just leave that body out there to rot!" she said.

"Quique is already on his way," another woman said with an air of superiority. "As soon as he finishes his route. That's what he told me when he dropped off my milk bottles." Quique was the town's milkman who finished his deliveries at around eight o'clock.

"Anyone know who the man is?" another guy asked, chewing on an unlit cigar.

Nobody knew. Heads rocked from side to side.

The roller-head wife said, "I heard he's not from here. Maybe he was a vagabond or a drunk. Maybe he was both."

"Where did you hear that?" the old man with the wrinkled face asked, not hiding his annoyance one bit. I could tell that things would soon escalate to name-calling. "No sea tan bochinchosa, señora. Why start spreading false stories?" he added.

"Mire, señor, you don't know me, so I would appreciate more respect. Or should I have my husband come and teach you some?"

The old man, contemplating an angry husband egged on by his woman's quick tongue, decided to turn around. He started walking in the direction where the dead body was supposed to be.

In silence, one by one, the group followed him. The slow procession climbed the small hill and entered a wooded area. I watched as they disappeared into the trees and bushes, thinking that all the fun had ended.

Carlito and I resumed our walk to school, but soon Guillermo blocked our path with a wild, excited look on his face.

"Are you guys crazy?" he asked. "Come on, let's go and see the body. How many times do you think we're going to get this opportunity? Stop acting like cobardes and let's take a look. Or are the two of you afraid of a dead man?"

How could we back out?

Besides, Guillermo was our leader, El Capitán.

We shrugged with indifference and followed him. I took out another piece of sugarcane and let the sweet juice run down my throat. Some of the adults looked back at us. "Get out of here," a few of them said in unison.

But Guillermo wouldn't have any of it. He ignored them and kept going, staying behind just in case they tried to send us back the way we came. Their small talk faded away into quick nods. The breaking of twigs and the dragging of feet could be heard, and a young woman complained that her sandals were getting heavier to walk in.

"That means she's a puta," Carlito said, covering his mouth with the back of his hand. "She's a whore. That's why her sandals are getting heavy—means she never made it with the dead man and her heart is getting heavy because of it."

I looked at Carlito, wondering where the hell he came up with such nonsense, and if he really expected that anyone would believe it. He'd also claimed that he saved the school bus from rolling down a hill and killing everyone inside just the month before. He hadn't elaborated on how he did it, yet he was adamant about it.

The group up ahead stopped in front of a clearing. A long, loud gasp came out of everyone's mouth at the same time. From where I stood I could see something on the ground. A few women turned their faces away and made the sign of the cross, and some of the old men removed their hats, either for respect or to hide whatever was on the ground.

The shock made them forget that three boys were mere inches away. Guillermo was the first to get a good look at what lay at the grown-ups' feet. Carlito and I inched our way over to him. In retrospect, I wish I had gone to school that morning instead of being such a follower. This changed after that day.

Thank God.

The dead man was about four feet away, his eyes still open. The whiteness around his pupils shone bright, contrasting with the deep purple bruises on his face. Brownish blood was caked in the open slashes on his neck and torso. His pants were pulled down to his ankles and there was a savage hole where his penis had been.

Most of the blood had been soaked up by the ground and washed away by the previous night's rain. I wanted to look away, but the brutality of his death was as fascinating as it was horrible. Then I saw something else that caught my attention, almost hidden by the bushes. I squinted to get a better look.

I saw a handle half-buried in the disturbed earth.

Sirens approached fast and the crowd began to disperse. I inched closer to where the handle was, and with one foot pushed it farther into the ground. Then I joined my friends. I walked down the hill without looking at them.

It had been two days since the discovery of the body. It gripped our small town in a web of suspicion and uneasiness. *There's a killer among us*, was the cry heard many times. *Maybe it was a wanderer and not one of us*, was the argument to fight back against the paranoia that had consumed everyone.

But I knew the truth.

I walked to school alone that morning and ignored Guillermo's and Carlito's calls to wait for them. I kept spinning the image of the handle in my mind as I pushed it into the ground. It was my father's machete handle, and I was sure that the blade was near the scene some-where.

I went through the motions of the day, yet I felt like an empty vessel with no spirit inside. My spirit never left the place where the man had found his death at the hands of my father.

I had recognized the man, regardless of his disfig-ured face. I hadn't known him well, but my father had brought him home just two weeks before.

They staggered in late that night, drunk and loud. So who was he? I didn't know for sure. I never knew his name. A stranger. Perhaps the lady with the rollers had been right—a wanderer or laborer that happened to be-friend my father.

And charmed my mother . . .

I saw him return twice, late at night after that first night, while my father was dead-to-the-world drunk. Mami had left the house and disappeared with him, only to return hours later. Always a few hours before my fa-ther woke up.

That's what she thought.

My father was a good faker when it was to his ad-vantage.

At age ten, in the so-called innocence of the 1960s, nothing wicked or carnal had ever crossed my mind—but I did have a vivid imagination. When school let out later that day, I slipped away from my friends and returned to the spot where the man had been killed. I went straight to the bushes.

The handle was still there.

In those days, police work was sloppy and not as thorough as it would become. I could still see dried blood and the impression the body had made in the ground. I pulled the handle out and looked around on all fours to make sure I hadn't missed anything.

My diligence was rewarded. About twenty minutes later, I found the steel blade from my father's machete. There were still streaks of dried blood on it. I took both pieces with me and went home, stashed them behind the latrine.

My father's drinking increased and his foulness and nastiness with it.

I heard the sound of flesh smacking flesh late one night, bestial groans from my father's throat. I knew damn well what was going on. My mother was being beaten and raped by the man she had vowed to honor and obey until death undid them apart.

She could no longer hide the bruises on her arms, legs, and face by combing her hair or by wearing long-sleeved blouses. I took all of this, just like my mother did, with silence. And after school every day—behind the latrine—I mended my father's machete.

And I planned.

The beatings my mother got nightly began to take their toll. She became a frightened and defeated creature. There was no shadow left of the woman I had loved so much. Her tears were my tears. Her pain was my pain. We became shells, spiritless shells.

As the coquís sang their sweet lullabies and the small town slumbered in a peaceful sleep one night, I slipped away from the house and went straight to the latrine. I'd planned for days and weeks. I waited for the bastard to come around the bend, on the familiar road where trucks drove by in the mornings and were chased by little boys.

I saw his silhouette under a weak moon, a black smear staggering along the road. I waited, hunched behind bushes, where I found some sugarcane forgotten by the boys.

I heard his boots dragging on the road, sending small pebbles skidding into the bushes. One of them tumbled, jumped into the air, and hit the raised machete blade.

I could smell the sweat and alcohol seeping out of his pores, even from there. I could smell his breath that came in and out in halting hiccups and loud, disgusting burps.

His bloodshot eyes popped out from their sockets when the sharp blade—*his* precious blade—slashed him along his neck, slicing his throat open. Blood shot out like a busted water pipe, and he pressed his fingers to the wound.

He staggered backward, then sideways, and the momentum knocked him forward. I swung the machete again, slicing half his face off. His knees buckled and he landed hard, still holding onto his throat and making gurgling sounds—for with severed vocal cords there were no screams of death. I buried the blade into his black heart with one final thrust and ran like a demon.

The morning sun rose above the mountains and the wind brought the aromas of a new day with it. Grandpa's rooster flapped his tired, old wings and stretched his scrawny neck—he crowed. I could hear soft snoring coming from my mother's room.

The peaceful sleep she had been denied for too long.

I smiled. *She will sleep better from this day forward*, I told myself.

Sirens approached from the distance, and I could hear the chattering of a nervous crowd gathering at the bend in the road. I pretended I was still sleeping when the first knocks came urgently on the door.

Originally written in English

SWEET FELINE

BY ALEJANDRO ÁLVAREZ NIEVES
El Condado

I'd been told that the security office at the Majestic was a labyrinth, like the ones in the movies. So when they took me there—handcuffed, held by the arm, disgraced—I lost myself in that sea of monitors and Internet servers, until I was left sitting in that little room. That's when I woke up to the reality of the situation: they were going to kick me out of the Majestic, after seventeen years working my ass off for this fucking hotel. The shift manager showed up fifteen minutes later, with his characteristic mafioso air, face serene and eyes unhinged. He entered the room and sat down facing me. A few seconds went by and he didn't say anything. I was quiet too. Like a gangster, he removed a cigarette from his pack and offered me one. I was scared shitless, so I started to blubber excuses: "My bad, man, she tricked me, I didn't see it coming." I was always careful, stuff like that never happened to me. He just wanted me to tell him everything before that dumb-ass Hermann showed up with a police officer. Because part of that whole theater would be meeting with the director of Security and an agent from the CIC—the night manager always wanted to be told everything, no matter what it was. If you stepped up and told the truth, he'd also step up and support the staff. If you didn't support the staff, the hotel was screwed. I won't lie, I didn't trust my boss, man. Because all of that sounds nice, camaraderie among men, that bullshit about not sticking your nose in anyone else's business—until someone sticks a knife in your back.

"Relax, Papi. Tell me everything. And then repeat the story in front of Hermann and the agent. I'll be with you the whole time. I got your back. Don't worry," he said.

Relax? . . . *How do you get to Jayuya? Take the back road*—that's what my grandpa always said. You get it? I had to make sure that the night manager would have my back, you know. It wasn't the first time that Security had interrogated me, nor was it the first time that a police detective had questioned me during an investigation. Being interviewed in the manager's office and being handcuffed and interrogated in a bunker are not the same thing. For the first time, I was the subject in question, and I had to know if this guy was going to have my back. It really fucked with me not knowing for certain that no matter what I said and what happened, the next day I'd head to the bellhop room, punch in, and go to work. That's how I earn a living, and I couldn't let any manager get in the way of that. So I had no choice but to tell him.

Her name was Candy, or that's what she said, you know, and she'd been staying in the Ocean Suites for three days. A blonde with a tight body, one of those rare girls from somewhere in the Southwest US: tall, blond, green eyes. Not more than twenty-five. Always in tropical clothes, but elegant, with a small tattoo of an infinity symbol on her right wrist and an Egyptian cross on her left. A sea of freckles sprinkled across her tits. From the time she stepped through the arch of the main entrance, she was throwing cash around left and right. Thirty bucks for Antonio to go get her luggage, three hundred as an appetizer for the girl at reception to give her an exclusive suite facing the sea. A hundred for Ortiz to bring up her luggage. Come on, the girl, being Southern, was a gravy train. When they dropped off her luggage, she just sat down on the balcony chair and called down to order a bottle of Cristal and some strawberries dipped in chocolate. Fifty bucks for room service, easy.

To top it off, she was nice. She smiled wide, her cheeks pocked with dimples. She strolled all around the terra-cotta marble of the lobby. She inspected the details in the wood, the lights, the assortment of orchids with a captivated expression, like some kind of hippie Indiana Jones—you know the way some women are, the way they act kind of dumb, but then all of a sudden they pull out the whip or put a bullet in you, eyeing you up and down like an aborigine. She talked to whomever she wanted whenever she wanted, guest or employee, it didn't matter. She asked about everything, from what your job was to how many kids you had, putting on an interested face. It was impossible to tell if she was really paying attention or if she was possessed by the coldest cynicism on the planet.

Something didn't add up, man. Nobody can be that happy. This was a twenty-something girl, swimming in cash, traveling alone to Puerto Rico, never having been there, not speaking a lick of Spanish. Spending like there's no tomorrow in the hotel stores, tossing cash around as if she were selling lottery tickets. And later, the evening transforming her into a sports car on the highway of youth. Out all night partying with the waitresses from the lobby, who were in her pocket before nine p.m. the day she arrived. Asking Antonio to bring bags of blow to her room. Who the hell snorts blow on their own like that? Renting a Ferrari to take a spin around Condado. Fuck, not even the old perverts who come down here twice a month do that. I don't know, brother, but all that craziness didn't add up for me, it made me look at her funny. The ones with fangs are always smiling, my old man used to say. So much courtesy smells fishy. And she must have noticed the mistrust on my face, because the only person that Candy Smith paid zero fucking attention to was me. What the fuck?

I figured this out on the afternoon of the fourth day of her stay. Three days of working. Three days in which I never got to bring her anything, three days without her even calling me at the bellstand to ask for the newspaper or to have her dirty clothes taken to the laundry. Fuck, I wasn't able to even take a pencil to that she-devil! Three days of not reaching my quota: a hundred bucks in tips. That's the minimum I need to be able to cover my bills for my apartment, car, the monthly fee at the school, and child support to my three kids. Three days in which I didn't even get to fifty. It was mid-September, the hotel was almost empty, and the only gravy train didn't even look at me by mistake. At one point she passed in front of the bellhop room and I swear on my mother that she stared right through me. But she didn't smile at me, not even a twitch of her lips to indicate she knew I was there, just the cold look of her green panther eyes. Thirty-four years and I still can't resist a pair of green eyes.

With all of that, I thought it was mere coincidence that she'd ignored me. Forget it, calm down. It's just that according to the laws of probability, fucking Candy would have to order something to her room, and I would be first in line to take it to her. Ah, but everything bad comes in bulk all at the same time, my old lady used to say. That afternoon I was first in line. And how could my knees not shake when that tigress appeared in the gallery on the way to the elevators, and suddenly I saw her coming toward me, her humble servant? It nearly gave me a heart attack when she turned to look at me for a few seconds with her feline eyes and then jerked them away. She went past, put something in Ortiz's hands, and whispered in his ear. I wasn't about to allow this to continue right in front of me, so I got technical: "That's mine, it's my turn." Ortiz knew it, and made a move as if to give me what he had in his hand, but she stopped him. "Not you, him!" the she-devil said, fixing me with those two backstabbing emeralds. Just like that, she turned and left. Fuck Candy—fuck Jolly Ranchers, Charms, Smarties, Hershey's, and M&M's! Fuck your mom's gofio. That little fucking gringa was guarding me worse than LeBron James, and she just threw a massive block. That night I went home with barely twenty bucks.

The night before she went back to Gringolandia, I showed up with smoke coming out of my ears. I knew that panther was taking off and I'd be left without any gravy. Everyone flaunted the loot they'd mooched off that ridiculous woman, and I was empty-handed. I even went around the lobby with my shirt unbuttoned, that's how much I wanted to be working that Saturday. I did my rounds. I went to the front desk and saw that less than ten rooms had been filled all afternoon and night. The housekeeping and maintenance boys went up to the presidential suite at seven to watch the Yankees game—they were in first place and the season was ending. "Bring some beers." I checked in with Security, but there was only one girl working, the same one as always. I went by housekeeping to see if the Colombiana was on that night, but she'd called in sick. A boring shift awaited me, broke and horny. No cash and left hanging. No way.

The call came late, around two in the morning, an hour before the end of my shift, while I was looking at the centerfold in *Primera Hora* with Ortiz in the bellhop room. It was Ortiz's turn, he was working the overnight shift, so I didn't even pay attention to the sound of the phone. He says it's for me. I go to the phone, laughing sarcastically. In hotels nobody calls you unless it's your wife, your ex, one of your bosses, or a family emergency. Everyone else comes by in person, to keep from being monitored. Turns out it was the lovely Candy. She called me by name: "Hi, Danny." She asked for two grams of blow, and for me to bring them to the room. I go see Antonio, the doorman. I put in the order.

I wait for the call and say the password of the week.

I am crossing the pool area by the beach and it's deserted, too empty. No guests fooling around hidden by the vegetation, no employees groping each other behind the bar, which was closed at that hour. It wasn't surprising. September was the time of skinny cows. But the Security staff weren't at their posts, and that wasn't quite so normal. Probably went up to watch the game too, dead as things were. Could be. Still, my internal alarms were going off. She hadn't invited any men into her room the whole time she'd been there. I found that out from the boys. This wasn't good. Even if it would've been cool to leave my mark on the sweet panther, all the bad vibrations had me on edge.

I arrived at the Ocean Suites complex and knocked on the door of room 223. Candy opened quickly, looked me up and down. She smiled at me for the first time, placing me under the spell of the dimples in her cheeks. My friend, she was wearing nothing but a bra and panties, made of that cloth that looks like tiger skin. What do they call it? *Animal print.* Exactly. Because the girl *is* animal print. At first I stayed there in the doorway, like a vampire waiting to be invited inside, not realizing that it was my blood that was going to be sucked. I don't know, I was enchanted by her jade eyes, and the next thing I remember is that I was beside her on the living room sofa drinking champagne and lifting a bump of coke to my nose on my car key. Then I proceeded to use the master key to cut out real lines. I lost count after the fifth hit. Then the heavy petting began, first an amazing kiss, then I went down her neck, down both arms, happily to her tits, starting to bite them softly. You know, that little game with the teeth somewhere between sucking and biting? Try it, man, it takes them right to the edge. It seemed like it was going well, because all of a sudden that Yankee grabbed me like a bear, lifted me, and threw me onto the bed like a lucha libre move. In two movements she took off my uniform and underwear. She lay down beside me and gave me another dose of the green magic, then stretched back and whispered in my ear: "Get on. Get on, cabrón."

But I am faithful to the Puerto Rican technique, so I spread her legs and began feeling around for that little bean that would get her squealing like a fat pig. The trembling and arching of her spine alerted me that I'd found it. The little bean that'll give her pleasure and get me even on my bills. So now I go to put my tongue down there; I play with it, I rub it, I tease it, as if it were a cherry limber, a cherry Jolly Rancher, taking my revenge on the sweet feline. And the she-devil moans, writhes, and floods like a broken dam. I keep punishing her, and she keeps on contorting until she can't take it anymore and asks for it with a shriek. "Stick it in, motherfucker!" You gotta stick it in when they ask for it, you know. And so it goes. I jump up, raise her legs, wind up, and head for home. Slow at first, so she feels how it goes in and knows what's coming, so she melts like the cheap candy she is. Then, little by little, I pick up the pace. I put my hand over her mouth while moving up and down with more and more intensity. She grabs two of my fingers and sticks them in her mouth, trying to grab the headboard with her other hand. And suddenly she springs forward and rips her nails across my spine like a cat on its back. I shake her off and push her down. I feel the blood running across my back. This always happens to me with the skinny girls, they all scratch when they fuck. Now that I have her like this, I say vengefully: "¡Ignórame ahora, puta! ¡Pasa de largo ahora, pendeja!"

It was like she knew Spanish, because the Yankee pulled back and gave me such a crack to the jaw that I fell back on the bed. "Fuck you! Leave me alone! I said no!" she screamed, and grabbed me around the neck with such force that I had to climb back on top of her. She slammed another fist into my jaw and I fell facedown on top of her. I was so embroiled in what was happening that I didn't realize someone was knocking on the door. Suddenly it opened and there they were, watching me.

"What the hell is wrong with you, crazy bitch? Turn around and let me show you who's in charge here."

Those were the words that the three security employees and the night manager heard from my mouth while standing witness to that cabaret show.

"Get him off me! He's raping me!"

That was when I felt them dragging me out into the living room. Then they gave me my clothes and uniform so I could put them on in the bathroom, where they locked me in for half an hour. No big deal. Candy fucked me over—she said she'd called me to collect her dirty clothes and that I came in and raped her without saying a word. At least that's what I heard from the other side of the wall. Obviously I could've asked them where the bag of dirty clothes was, where the order was. But there's no margin of error here, man. Even if something isn't your fault, you get screwed over. Tell me how you could possibly explain that to the hotel manager, to a fucking cop. There was no catching a break, the axe had fallen. Hotels are a reality show—it's not what happens at home, it's whatever the producers put on for people to see. And what they saw was me on top of a guest, with marks of violence on my body. I was fried. They cuffed my hands behind my back right there and took me to Security through the entrance to the restaurant that opened onto the pool. The last picture I have in my mind of Candy Smith is the little smile of triumph at the corners of her mouth, and the green that sparked from her eyes when the night manager told her in English not to worry, that all of her expenses would be covered by the hotel. "We're going to take care of you, miss." Fuck all candies. I've never had a sweet tooth.

It was clear that the cabrón night manager wouldn't have my back. I don't even know if I should tell you that none of this is personal. Hotels are run like the mafia, everything for the good of the business, not for the good of those occupying it, not for the good of those who enjoy it. They're all guinea pigs. What matters is how much cash you make them and how much cash the guests spend. The rest is bullshit. Turns out the dumb-ass Hermann isn't such a dumb-ass. He was in the next room watching my "confession" on a video monitor. When I stopped talking, he opened the door and came in with an employment termination form in his hands. They didn't let me quit, the fuckers. If I'd quit, at least I would've been paid seventeen years' severance. I didn't find out anything else about the girl. Nobody tells me anything. Everyone from the hotel avoids me. This was a month and a half ago. And here I am, waiting for my paycheck.

"And you, what're you doing here? Get mugged over at Santurce Plaza too?"

"No, I'm chilling. It's just the hotel is in rough shape and they laid us off until November. But the axe comes and goes, I got a couple months of unemployment to even the score."

"Man, you don't have to tell me twice. But don't say any of that to the officer, loco. There are fewer federal funds for the people all the time."

"Relax, one of the supervisors is a buddy of mine. We go way back."

"Ah, good. How lucky . . . Hey, what's the name of the night manager at the Majestic?"

"Melecio. Carlos Melecio."

"Ay! It was you with the con artist. Damn, loco, everyone in the industry knows that story, dude."

"What? Don't mess with me, man."

"They booted Melecio too. Turns out the gringa was an underwear model and a professional con artist. She'd charged more than a hundred thousand dollars in jewelry and clothes to her hotel account. When everything went down, the hotel didn't realize. The trick is that they don't realize what's happened until she's already on the plane heading home. She did the same thing at the Conquistador, the Marriott, and the Intercontinental too. I thought you guys knew about her. Fuck! I didn't know the bellboy was you. Damn, everything's so fucked up."

"You're not messing with me, right?"

"No, I swear. Last week I ran into Inés, one of the girls from the lobby at the Cactus, at four in the morning and she told me everything. I can't believe it, man . . . Ah, that's my number. See you. Good luck, man. Take care."

And so I stayed in that chair, watching as my buddy from Santurce Plaza went in to talk to his case officer, wondering what other hotel Carlos Melecio had hidden in.

I went outside to smoke a cigarette. I came back quickly because it was hotter than hell. When I got the paperwork from a little old lady, I wondered what story I could invent to convince the officer to accept my case, when I couldn't put down the only legal employment I'd had in more than fifteen years as a reference.

THINGS TOLD WHILE FALLING

BY YOLANDA ARROYO PIZARRO

San José

> *So many things begin and perhaps end as a game.*
> —Julio Cortázar, "Graffiti"

1.

You play at identifying buildings to avoid the anxiety that landing always causes. There you are, right in the middle of the airplane's gut, aisle seat. From there you watch, turning your neck from side to side, and spread yourself into that metal bird's extremities. Left wing and right wing; engines to the right and left; identification lights off—it's daytime—to the left and the right.

A therapeutic late-afternoon sun threatens to leave you blind, keeping you from enjoying the descent. You curse the blind man to the left, in the window seat, who cares little about looking out of it. If only they'd given you that seat. You also curse the abundantly white Afro of the old lady sitting in the seat next to the right window. The mass of her messy hair blocks all visibility. You move restlessly about in your seat, sometimes stretching your neck, bobbing up and down, rolling your shoulders, trying to play the game. The game that calms you, keeps you from falling into mania.

You spot the first identifiable place: Palo Seco, an energy plant that supplies electricity to various towns, which exploded once when you were little. The fire could be seen all the way from Las Vegas, Bay View, even from Amelia, the neighborhood where you grew up. No one was implicated in that "accidental" incident, blessed ode to the impunity of creole terrorism. Fuentes Fluviales, as they were previously called; now the AEE in concert with the AAA, investigated by the FBI. You spell them out to see if you remember what each letter stands for—it's part of the game. Not getting nervous is always the primary objective. Fucking landing.

You keep playing at identifying structures. The second one: Los Molinos, some concrete plants where they manufacture purine, grain, and other contaminants. You also identify the barges at the dock, the cranes, the containers. Some of them say *Sealand*, others *Navieras de Puerto Rico*. Your uncle worked all his life for an abusive business just like that one, until he ended up with Alzheimer's, Parkinson's, and a pension that barely provided enough to buy the essentials: eggs, milk, bread. Never meat. Never some good chops or steaks. Los Molinos, even today, continues to erode the health of many people, without the affected or the witnesses ever saying or doing anything. Without anybody protesting.

Plaza Las Américas, the center of everything. From Santa Cruz, Saint Thomas, and Monserrat—where a volcano spouts ash on its leeward side every ninety-some days—people come from all over the Antilles to buy things and lose themselves in the largest commercial center in the Hispanic, Anglo-Saxon, and Francophone Caribbean. "The people from the little islands" is what they call those individuals with ordinary features. You remember well that during your childhood, your grandma called them *madamos*. Actually, that's what she called the really dark blacks, the purple blacks; the ones who did or didn't wear turbans. Blacks blacker than you, with gigantic noses and protruding lower lips.

Teodoro Moscoso Bridge. You promise yourself you'll look up who the hell that guy was on Wikipedia, because the truth is, neither you nor anybody you've asked knows. You've always imagined that it has something to do with Moscoso Pharmacy, the one you frequented as a kid on the way to the Cantaño boat launch, where one time they found a half-dozen dogs with their throats slit, and no one immediately responsible despite the fact that the suspects walked around at school quietly singing: *Under my house, there's a dead dog. The one who says eight, will eat it off their plate, one, two, three, four, five, six, seven . . .*

Approaching the bridge you get unnerved, because you've reached that point of arrival. You stretch your neck even farther, and the old lady with the white Afro notices. She gestures to you with her hand, asking if you want her seat. You say yes. So she stands and you stand too, and from a distance, the flight attendant scolds you because you're supposed to remain seated, the plane is about to land. When the warning ends, you're already clutching the window.

You fasten your seat belt. You pull out your digital camera because you like to take photos of the landing. You count in silence and breath rhythmically. You're about to pass over the booth of the excessively expensive toll that opens onto Avenida Central, and everything ceases to be Lilliputian. First photograph. You inhale and exhale. Now you count the flags of the damned United States and the blessed Island of Enchantment fixed to the bridge as they grow larger. Photograph. You inhale and exhale. You count the little houses on the water in San José, all of them half-fallen into the lagoon that's deminiturizing in front of your eyes. You inhale. A boat and you replicate Gulliver's gaze. You exhale. Flash. A San Juan police boat and you are Micromegas. You breathe in. Two kayaks. One bright blue and the other apple green. You breathe out. A jet ski. Another photo. You inhale. Another boat, the coast guard this time. A sequence of flashes. A police helicopter hovers far away, and you imagine it'll wait until the air traffic clears to approach. You hold your breath. The mangrove. You turn off the camera's flash and hold down the shutter to lengthen the sequence. The mangrove increasing in size and the bushes with splayed roots drinking from the pestilent lagoon. A body. A floating body. Your finger pressing the button gets nervous, but keeps shakily shooting the target. A woman floating in the water with breasts and downy pubis exposed. Her face so far away from you, from your plane, and lifeless. Zoom in on every detail, zoom in on every new horror. Arms extended, like the wings of the aircraft, but she doesn't fly. A woman who doesn't fly. Increase zoom to 60X Optical by 2000X Digital. Hands removed from those arms at the wrist; surgically severed without pain or glory. They're gone. A woman, dead and incomplete. A corpse that screams of violence and welcomes you back to your homeland, after ten years of absence.

2.

You fall.

In the end you fall across the surface of the planet, which turns out to be the same as the surface of your homeland. You fall, landing and floating, intrigued and alone. So alone. Falling things have the significance of lost things, of abandoned things, of things invented to stave off madness, of the sudden daring that's preceded by fear. A desperate need to tell of fallen things that will later keep you company is more than right and necessary.

You start breathing again when you pick up your bags at carousal ten. You pause and look at the screen of your camera where your photos have been stored. You zoom in and out to see every detail. You only know what's been explained over the loudspeaker and by passengers with Internet access on their cell phones. Minimal information regarding the discovery, the crime scene, or the investigation. Everyone tried to move to the windows, to see what could be seen. You were one of the lucky few who caught a glimpse of the dead girl laid out like that—lifeless skin in its greatest splendor. Inert skin on an island that leaves so many alone, so many orphaned, widowed, and dispossessed. The rest of the travelers have resigned themselves to the speculations of those who saw something. There's another hubbub inside Luis Muñoz Marín International Airport. Everyone is talking about it, speculating about the stranded people who won't be able to make their flights out of the country because of the traffic jam. They've closed off various roadways including, of course, the one that connects to the bridge. The family members who would certainly be coming to pick up the arriving travelers wouldn't be there either, as they haven't been allowed through. No one was coming to get you anyway; you weren't going to be received by anybody. A total helplessness impregnates the air, an ode to detachment. So witnessing those who are stranded gives you great pleasure.

3.

You leave your bags at a fleabag hotel in Isla Verde and get back in the rental car. You arrive at the San José police station from the opposite side of the bridge, coming in on Milla de Oro, behind Plaza las Américas. Your pithy journalism courses at Universidad del Sagrado Corazón provide the key to getting inside. You remove the little notebook and pencil, conveniently located in the front pocket of your striped shirt, identify yourself as a press correspondent, and show your driver's license with the New York City logo. The checkpoint officer, not really paying attention, lets you pass. Already mingling with a small group of reporters, you simply fall in line and listen. Listen and pretend to write in your little notebook. Simulating professional interest, looking up and down. Listening with great care. Finding out as much as possible.

4.

At the funeral, you meet the dead girl's mother, her sisters, her uncles, aunts, and cousins, who cry facing the casket, to the beat of a rhythm like a jukebox bolero. You add and subtract, and the obvious notable absence is the husband, a man originally from Saint Martin—he's the only one not in attendance. The "best friend" is there, and she cries desperately, as if something valuable has been torn away from her. To those who ask, you say you were classmates with the dead girl. *At Colegio San Vicente?* someone sporadically inserts, and you immediately nod yes.

Later that day you discover another interesting possibility: the "best friend" of the dead girl, a lesbian, hasn't come to the burial. Everyone speculates. You decide to interview friends and acquaintances, in groups. Sometimes together and sometimes alone. Like the older sister, who talks about the pain one feels when something very dear is taken away. She also talks about the odyssey of staying single at this age, in such a mundane society, so frivolous, so machista, so full of double standards. That afternoon, without wanting to, your mouth and hers find one another. She cries and you're amazed to be swallowing her tears while kissing her. You know what it is to lose someone. You know what it is to be left with nobody. You know it very well.

Over the nine days of the novena celebration, you've gained the confidence of Violeta's older sister. That is the dead girl's name: Violeta. You go to the movies, you eat lunch in the Plaza Food Court, you even go to the General Police Station to give testimony regarding one of the suspects. When the detective in charge of the investigation interrogates you, you tell him about your concerns regarding the participation of the lesbian lover in that horrific crime. You insist on the strangeness of that supposed friend who's now disappeared. And with great skill you delineate your hypothesis of the amputated hands. From your perspective—that of a man dedicated to collecting stamps, baseball cards, and memorabilia about *The Divine Comedy*—severed hands represent the feminine genitalia. You explain how gay women use their hands to give and receive pleasure: the fingertips and fingernails to tease; the palm to rub; the stem of the extremity to caress; two, three, and even four fingers to penetrate; a brush of knuckles in obvious seduction; inserting a full fist in clear domination; the end. That's why the dead girl Violeta was killed, you say. Her lesbian lover—when she found out Violeta wouldn't get a divorce, and that she also very possibly had another male lover—went crazy. Violeta, the best friend from high school, inseparable even after college, deep down wanted to end that affair, but the other girl's rage wouldn't allow it. She'd rather kill her than not have her for herself.

5.

So when, three days later, the paper publishes the news that Violeta's widower has turned himself in to the authorities, you don't give it any credibility. You're unconvinced that the grief-stricken husband had it in him to cut off her hands, despite the sensationalistic details: he hit her when he drank, cut her with kitchen knives, with scissors, skewered her with screwdrivers—and one night, she hit back. She got tired of it. Defending herself cost her her life.

You look at the photos from your digital camera that you've already had developed and printed. You decorate several walls of your temporary home. The lagoon, the mangrove, the rescue boat, the body.

Found bodies make silent speeches. The demise of that human being is fully explained by the exposed sequence of details of that found body. All that's missing is the translator, who reveals the linguistic code and explains it. You feel that you are the translator. Will there be signs of lost love, of diminished feeling, in the energy surrounding a lifeless body?

You stop seeing her sister because you intuit that her whole family is a fiasco, a string of deceitful blacks, blacker than you. What an evil thing to lie to the citizenry about a crime, just to have it cleared up. You're convinced the husband is innocent. So in the end, Violeta's death was well deserved.

Her pathetic sister, melodramatic and blubbering, is just like your few remaining family members. Your grandma—thank God she's six feet under—was right: one can never trust a madamo.

PART III

Never Trust Desire

TURISTAS

BY ERNESTO QUIÑONEZ

Dos Hermanos Bridge

For Edward Rivera

I came to San Juan because Mama said my father, a certain Salvador Agron, lived here. "Remember, Julio, only ask of him what is due to us. What he never gave us." Mama was leaving this world, and with a sense of urgency she passed on the family inheritance by handing me the envelope. I never put much stock into it. But I loved Mama, and so I promised to find my father.

I was staying at the Sheraton Puerto Rico Hotel & Casino, and in the afternoon I went looking for him. Scaling up hills covered with multicolored colonial houses, cobblestone streets, and tons of tourists, most from cruise ships docked by the Malecón. The only pictures I had of my father were from when he was a teenager, when he acquired his famous name.

I spotted three old men sitting outside, drinking coffee by a café.

"Have any of you seen an old man named Salvador Argon, also known as the Capeman?" I asked in Spanish.

"You came to San Juan looking for an old man?" one

of them answered in Spanish. "The whole town is old."
And they laughed together.

I continued walking. The humidity never bothered
me. I expected to find him in some corner drunk and
lost. I walked all around Old San Juan. Lit a candle for
Mama at the cathedral. The cult of Mary is not in my
bones.

Exhausted, I gave up as night was approaching. I
took a taxi back to the Sheraton.

I replayed this search the next day with no luck.

On the third day he rose from the dead; I received
the call. It was a female voice, speaking in English.

"You are looking for the Capeman?"

"Yes," I said anxiously.

"Why?"

"Who is this?" I asked.

"Meet me tomorrow at the San Juan Gates, where
the fishermen are." And she hung up.

Whoever she was, she knew him by his famous
name. So she knew what he had done.

My father was born in Mayagüez and had been shuffled
from the island to New York City by his parents as many
times as he would later be shuffled from juvenile detention to juvenile detention, from prisons to asylums and
back to prisons.

He came from a time when the New York City streets
belonged to teenage gangs. My father was president of
the Vampires. Like many members, he had dropped out
of school, left his mother, and then rented a five-dollar-
a-week single-room occupancy on the Upper West Side.

The night of the playground incident was a Saturday. All over the West Side of New York City, from the 100s down to the 60s, the large population of Puerto Ricans who lived there before gentrification, before the cleaning up of Needle Park, were taking in the street life. Radios blasting salsa. Everyone looking for someone to love and be loved in return. Everyone cooling off from a summer heat wave.

It was around nine o'clock when word arrived that some kids from a white gang named the Norsemen had beaten up a Puerto Rican member of the Vampires. As president of the gang, my father called up all the Puerto Rican members and told them to meet at the playground on 46th Street and Ninth Avenue. Some came walking. Others took the bus. My father jumped the turnstiles, hopped on the 1 train, got off at 42nd Street, and walked west. He was a Vampire and so he wore a cape. In his hands a dagger, along with years of anger, betrayal, abuse—a wealth of tragedies from his young life just waiting for a reason to be set free. When my father and his Vampires assembled at the playground it was midnight. The lampposts were broken. Hanging out by the swings were these two white boys. It was a moonless New York neighborhood known back then as Hell's Kitchen.

"Hey, no gringos in this playground!" my father yelled. The two white boys ran but my father and his Vampires chased and fell on them. My father tackled one of the boys, threw him down on the pavement, and started screaming at his face: "This is *our* playground. No Norsemen! No white Norsemen!" My father wielded his dagger. Began stabbing the white boy and then the other boy . . . but these were not the Norsemen. They were just white kids hanging out.

Bleeding a river of red, the first white boy made it to the entrance of a tenement building. He knocked on the door of some old lady. She quickly recognized him as a boy from the neighborhood. The old lady kneeled down and held the bloodied boy in her arms as if she wanted to give him what was left of her own life. He in turn looked up at her eyes and tried to say something but died in her arms.

The other white boy made it to his nearby tenement. He managed to drag himself up a flight of stairs and to his apartment. His mother opened the door and saw her bloodied son coughing like a broken radiator. She held her son as he died in the hallway.

This happened a long, long time ago, when my father was just a fourteen-year-old kid. New York City had never seen anything like this. My father made the cover of *Newsweek*. Was in *Time* and all over the papers. The media wanted his blood. Called him the Capeman. He was sentenced to the chair but was pardoned at the last minute and did sixteen years.

Many years afterward, a legendary and wealthy musician wanted access to my father's life story. This guy wanted to produce a multimillion-dollar Broadway musical based on my father's life. The musician went looking for my father too, like I am looking for him today, but all he found was Mama and a twelve-year-old me. The musician gave Mama a piece of paper; it was a legal contract. It stated that they were setting aside a lot of money in an escrow account. Should my father ever show up, the money would be waiting for him. The Broadway show went on, though Mama never saw it. She held onto that piece of paper like it was a lottery ticket. She kept the contract safe and dry for years. "Remember, Julio," she said to me on her death bed, "only ask of him what is due to us. What he never gave us."

The gates of San Juan are lovely, but they frightened me. They are there to lock you out. To deny you access to the city. To tell you that you are a pirate. An outsider from Spanish Harlem, the mainland. A tourist and not a true Puerto Rican from the island. When I arrived at the huge red doors, I did not enter. I stayed standing there looking out toward the sea. I was afraid that for some reason I would not be let back into San Juan, that I'd be left out among the iguanas and stray cats that roam El Morro all night and day. What scared me the most was that the Capeman might be on the other side.

"Are you going to just stand there or come help me fish?" she asked, not ten feet away from the gates.

"Hi," I said, "my name is Julio."

"I don't want to know your name. You came looking for my father?"

"*Your* father?"

"I have my net and pole over there," she pointed with her chin. "Come help me."

She was young, much younger than I was. She was lovely beyond anything, as if she had been assembled by a committee of men. She was sweaty. Wearing shorts and her long, long hair hid her behind when she walked in front of me. I quickened my pace for us to be side by side. I studied her face to see if I saw my father or myself in her. It was a stupid thing to do since I had never seen him. Just pictures of when he was the Capeman.

"Caldo de pez tastes so good," she said. "Touristy restaurants buy them from me. All I need is to catch one today and I'll have enough money for a month."

We walked toward a small inlet marina. There were many fishermen. From the boardwalk's platform stemming from El Morro, one could see the large fish swimming below.

"With you here next to me, the men won't be able to take the best spots for themselves. They'll see you and make way for me." She elbowed her way between two men who, annoyed, saw me standing behind her and left her alone. She then baited her pole and casted it out to sea. I could see that there were fish just a few feet away from us. "Those are no good," she said, knowing full well what I was thinking, "too skinny." She didn't have a hat or anything to cover her head and the sun was beating down on me. Even the men had covered their heads. "Why are you looking for my father?"

"Because if it's the same man, you are my sister."

But she didn't bat an eye. She continued to wield her pole, jiggling it, hoping to get a bite. "Do you know how many brothers I have? All from him. Do you see any of them trying to help me feed him?"

"I want to help you," I responded. "I have something for him."

She quickly took her eyes off the sea. "Give it to me," she demanded more than asked. She held the pole with one hand and stuck out the other toward me. "Give it to me and I'll give it to our father."

"Can you take me to him?"

"What is it that you have for him?"

I wasn't about to tell her. It was a long story. And I was not sure if she was telling me the truth.

"If you want to see the Capeman," she had both hands back on the pole, "you have to roam the streets of Old San Juan at night. That viejo only comes out late at night."

I had been searching for him only in the daytime; somehow she knew this.

"You'll find him by a tourists store that sells Cuban cigars under the counter," she said.

"What's your name?"

"Magaly."

I found him. Standing outside the cigar store on Calle Fortaleza, late at night, just like Magaly had said. He was wearing his cape. He was old but he was so tall that it gave him the appearance of having a lot of life left in him. He was light-skinned, almost white, with hazel eyes. The eyes saw me and smiled, and it was in the way he called me *papo* that I knew he felt comfortable both on the mainland and on the island.

"You see, papo, many people don't know me because I made myself invisible." He laughed a little laugh and he had a huge gap between his big front teeth. I saw that his cape was really worn out, the satin fading. His pants were thin too, as was his shirt, both fabrics disappearing into strings. His hair was long, parted in the middle, and held together with a rubber band. He reminded me of a broken-down Jesus Christ, ragged and old, whose disciples had long ago deserted him.

"My name is Julio," I said.

"Yes, I know." He peered at the night sky as if he had lost something there. "I gave you that name." His tone and his slumped shoulders told me he was harmless. No longer that kid who had killed people.

"I'd like to begin again. But you see, I can't do that, papo. So I live here in the night now and I try and forget, you know?"

"My name is Julio," I repeated because I didn't want him to keep calling me *papo*.

"Okay, papo, Julio," he said and smiled a bit. "Your sister told me you have something for me?"

"Yes, I have me. Your son." I don't know what I expected of him. I myself felt very little love. This was the first time I had ever seen him, talked to him. Why would I think he would feel any different?

"A son is always a good thing," he said with some joy, but no excitement.

"Mama is dead." I felt a pang of sadness just by saying this. I saw how it hurt him too. We were outside, on the sidewalk, with insects flying around us and drunken tourists walking by. He sat down on the warm cement and held his heart. I kneeled down and grabbed him because he was about to topple over in a sitting position. For the first time I saw his face up close. His eyes were faint glimmers in a nest of wrinkles.

"I'm sorry." I helped him get back up, leaned him against the wall of the cigar shop. "She didn't suffer."

"No, no, it's okay." He crouched now, hunching his shoulders like he was humbling himself. Like I've seen many tall people do when they feel inferior for being so tall. "I loved your mother," he said in almost a whisper, "I did love your mother." But no tears rolled down his face.

"But you left us and never came back." I had little sympathy for him. I was here only for Mama. "You left us."

He didn't look at me but at the night sky, as if he could find the past there. Then he looked at the concrete below us. A cricket was hopping by. Then he looked at the taxis driving tourists. Then at the night sky again, as if he wasn't sure where to start. When he did face me, his hazel eyes were huge like on an Egyptian's coffin at the Met. He scanned my face like nervous radar, deciding if he should answer.

"I needed to go," he placed a hand on my shoulder, "I needed to live in the darkness." His eyes were watery and his nose was running. "After what I did to those kids. The light, Julio, it shames me." And he embraced me. I embraced him too.

I took him back with me to the Sheraton Puerto Rico Hotel & Casino. I wanted to talk to him all night about many things, as if in one night I could make up for decades of his absence. I felt happy when we reached the hotel; he placed an arm around me and excitedly told people, "This is my son." He kept proudly saying this all night, to anyone who passed us, so that all could hear: "This is my son." That night he told me everything about how he became the Capeman. The killings of which most I already knew. Everything he said I had heard or read about, but hearing it from him made it all part of my life too, by being his son.

One night we went swimming at the nearby San Sebastian beach. It was there, when I tasted the salt of the Caribbean, that I felt he was truly my father.

"When you swim this sea," he said while we were in the water, the air cooling my temples, "you don't feel poor."

I knew I had to give him the envelope. All he had to do was sign it, show proof of who he was, and he'd have more money than he'd ever need.

"In America we could never taste the salt of the sea and feel the heat of the island, so we felt poor, we *were* poor, but here, Julio, I'm rich with nothing but my island."

I had stayed in San Juan for two weeks. Two weeks with my father talking at night, as he only came out at night. We talked about many things, catching up on our lives. Soon, my vacation time was over. I would need to go back to work. My intention was to go see him before I took the plane. Tell him about the contract and give it to him. Let him know I would send money so he could return to New York City. Stay with me while he straightened out and collected the money that the wealthy musician had set aside for him. And then it would be up to him.

At the Sheraton desk I received the checkout bill.

"He said many times he was your father. You're his son, right?" the hotel clerk said. I was being billed for thousands of dollars in casino gambling. "You are his son? And he was always with you?"

I had not stepped one foot in the casino, but he had. Many times, under my name and room number.

Before taking a cab to the airport I went looking for Magaly; I knew where I'd find her.

"You and him got me pretty good," I said. She was fishing the sea in a terrible spot since the men had taken all the good ones. "What's his real name?"

"Listen," she replied, continuing to hold her fishing pole steady, "everyone here is trying to make a living, okay? This island is poor. You are all tourists. Even if you are Puerto Rican, you don't live on the island; you are a tourist, and because of that, you have more money than us."

She wasn't going to tell me anything. She might really be his daughter. But it didn't matter.

"Magaly . . ." I handed her the contract. The piece of paper that Mama had kept for so many years, hoping that our ship would one day come in and like Columbus we would find riches. "Tell him that if he can play the part of the Capeman as well as he played it with me, there's money for him and you."

Boarding the plane, I could not get Mama's words out of my head: *Remember, Julio, only ask of him what is due to us. What he never gave us.* The plane took off and slowly Puerto Rico became a dot in an endless blue sea, and I knew I had obeyed her. Flying into that night sky, Mama was alive and I understood why she had held onto him even when she was leaving a world that would now and forever mean nothing to her. I was happy and felt less alone. I looked out the window; the stars were in my face again and I was sitting on Mama's lap like an obedient child.

Originally written in English

Y

BY JOSÉ RABELO
Santurce

Y ou think of Samira with a kind of guilty feeling—the best student, the most promising girl in the twelfth grade—now missing. Optimistically, you don't believe she's dead; she has just disappeared, location unknown.

You look at her photos on Facebook: one with her boyfriend, El Gato, murdered weeks earlier in the Manuel A. Pérez projects, that older boy who came to pick her up every afternoon in an old Mercedes-Benz.

You remember your student, her caramel face, long black hair, and the mole on her right elbow in the shape of a cockroach. That's how she described it, anyway. *Maestro, have you ever seen a cockroach wearing a wig? Well, look, there's one right here.* Then she took your right hand and made you feel the texture of her birthmark.

Again you think of her with a kind of guilty feeling, because you never talked to her about the dangers of the street. Combinatorial operations; absolute values; linear and quadratic equations; inverted functions; variable isolations; ratios and proportions—advanced mathematics doesn't allow room for other subjects.

Nobody's heard from her for two weeks. Her mother

suffers at home; she's all run out of tears. A long-time widow, and now she's lost her daughter too, that's what Señora Vélez, the social worker, said. Samira went out and didn't come back, just like that—a purebred puppy lost in the wild jungle of Río Piedras.

The students didn't know anything either.

Best case, she went off with a new boyfriend, said one of the boys in the classroom.

El Gato got her hooked on the meat. Who knows, someone might've kidnapped her to steal her kidneys, a goth girl suggested. *Sorry . . . not to be so morbid. She could've just left the country with someone to go become a dancer, everyone knows Samira was into that nonsense,* she continued.

That girl is dead, said a Pentecostal girl, *so she can't snitch on El Gato's killers.*

Her name always struck you as attractive: Samira. You even looked it up in the dictionary once. *Samira: of Islamic origin, a woman who tells stories at night, a female entertainer.* You look at her Facebook photos again. She's dressed as a belly dancer, in a black-and-gold costume covered with small metallic bells; everyone applauded when she won the talent show. You saw her leave with El Gato after the show that Thursday night, and you remember that she didn't come back until the following Monday.

You can't relax at home; an inaudible call compels you to leave the comfort of your apartment. You want to find the equation that will solve this mystery, and you wish for a new use of polynomial functions that would decode Samira's location. You long to touch the oblong mole on her elbow again, to determine how chance had planted it on her young skin.

* * *

You get on the train at Sagrado Corazón to see the city by night. It dawns on you that the map on the wall resembles a folded arm: the shoulder in Santurce, the elbow in Río Piedras, the hand in Bayamón. At the elbow you enter the subterranean part of the route—the underground, an inferno. You can't see the urban landscape; the windows reveal only darkness. You catch your reflection in the glass. You haven't shaved recently, so you look like a vagrant, a drunk sick with dengue fever. You don't see Samira. You get off the train and wander through the streets filled with bookstores, ruined buildings, bars, walls covered in urban art, the street dormitories of junkies recently introduced to the alternative life, and murals of dogs and cats. Deep down you consider the probability of running into Samira. If you found her, you'd ask her why she wanted to disappear. A homeless man tries to bum a cigarette; you say you don't smoke. *Asshole*, he says without resentment, staggering off down the street. If you found her, you wouldn't question her, you'd offer to help her—after all, you're just her teacher, not her father or relative—and you'd notify the social worker. Down a dark street, you see a man pull out his cock, moving it like a dead serpent. *This is what you're looking for, daddy, come get it, it's not easy to find around here.* You act like you don't see or hear him. You come to the public square. Cops remove a handcuffed man from a patrol car and take him into the station. Nobody would care if you found her—let her live however she wants, die however she wants, disappear however she wants. At that elbow on the map,

Río Piedras, you squash a cockroach on the ground near the station.

That night you dream of Samira: you find her in the classroom dressed in the black-and-gold outfit from the talent show; she's the teacher, you, the only student in a room illuminated by black candles. From a desk you watch her, glowing, self-absorbed, solving equations on the chalkboard. She turns around to begin class; the bells ring in the background. *This is what we call the inverse ratio, with the constant* Ω. *This kind of ratio also appears in natural processes and phenomena, for example . . .* In the middle of her explanation, a gust of wind slips in through the recently opened door. All the candles go out; the moon provides the only illumination for what comes next. El Gato enters and undresses in front of a silent Samira. She keeps looking at you, as if wishing to continue the math lesson. He's in front of her, naked, his skin covered with tattoos—skulls, tombstones, feline sex acts, men with pistols in place of their genitals, and women with breasts like curled-up cats. He strikes her and throws her on the floor. She seems to enjoy the beating. You stay motionless, paralyzed. You don't want to stand; watching her suffer makes you feel good, so you watch her enjoy it, smiling passively, bleeding from the nose. El Gato positions her on the desk to take her. He's panting, they're panting, moaning, licking each other. You feel them licking your neck, and then you're panting, it's you moving on top of her, you feel your cock inside of her. El Gato is no longer there—you're El Gato now—your arms spread on the desk, which creaks, and your arms are cat legs. You growl, you meow, and your tail quivers with pleasure. She sticks her claws into your chest. The pain wakes you up.

You don't turn on the light to shower. You scrub your body vigorously as you try to remove the filth from your skin and your brain. You've seen cats clean themselves with their tongues, passively, parsimoniously, with all the time in the world, but yours is not a cat bath—it's tense, exaggerated. But the water doesn't eradicate the filth you feel, the dirt you harbor. It runs bloody in the darkness, down the drain that's darker still.

When morning comes you have no desire to get up, to go back to the school. You decide to stay home with the memory of the dream, the sensation of claws embedded in your chest, and the thought of Samira presenting a report on inverse trigonometric functions. She herself was inverse: she wasn't a normal adolescent; she acted like an adult, a teacher, erudite. She spoke more than the rest of the kids combined, and her conversation was substantive. *Maestro, if so many people live happily off government benefits without needing to study, why do us kids have to study so much? Maestro, if God knows everything, why did He create the devil?*

That question goes beyond the scope of mathematics, you would always answer.

You look like a vagrant now. You watch the news again, flip through the channels, peer out the apartment's front and back windows, and look through the newspaper. You read every page and inspect every photo, but you don't find Samira. Your hands are dirty, so you clean them with your tongue, passively, parsimoniously, with all the time in the world. Math is good for nothing—nothing in this life—it doesn't help you live well, or be born, it doesn't help yield high probabilities of ending up with an good family, and when you die it won't give you one extra microsecond.

The students give you a surprising reception. *Maestro, you don't look so good. Are you sick? You look like you're about to die. Maestro, we have news for you,* says one of the boys in the classroom. *Look at this picture.* You see the façade of a notorious bar called Y. Stories of killings that have happened there have been in the papers and on the news before. You think of "Y" as one of the protagonist variables in an equation on the chalkboard. *Some of my friends saw her there last night . . . She's a total star, a sensation, the little jewel of the business, the most popular whore. Maestro, can you go save her?*

You let the night enter you as you board the train at Sagrado Corazón. You no longer care that the map of your trajectory resembles a folded arm, but you do remember the mole in the shape of a cockroach on Samira's elbow; you enter the underground at that elbow. The urban landscape is unimportant, you think, seeing the long beard of a sick, drunk Zeus. You don't see Samira. You exit the train and enter the street amid the shadows and decaying odors, where cat-sized rats run by. Deep down you think about the probability of forgetting Samira. A kid offers you cocaine. You tell him that you're not interested. *Fuck yourself,* he says without fear. You want to go home. Down a dark street you see two women kissing, and you act like you don't notice. You arrive at Y.

Some men enter with the tranquility of coming home; you long to go to your own home. *I'm ridiculous*, you can't stop thinking. The large, red Y outside invites you in, as if you'll find the answer to the equation you're trying to solve.

You drink two beers in one hour—the last one already tastes bitter. You listen to the noise; the salsa; the solicitations of older women: you can do everything for this much; the proposals of little girls; none of them is Samira. You feel tricked; it's impossible that you'd find one of your students here. With her intelligence she's guaranteed a promising future. Samira would become an upstanding citizen. You think about ordering another beer, but instead decide to pay, leave a tip, and get out of there. You make your way through the patrons who're there to have a good time.

Back on the train you hear the faraway click of high heels. A shadow approaches with a distinct glow around her hair, like a character with a halo from the calendar of saints. She moves sensually, the sashay of hips possessed by tropical music—you can almost imagine the salsa playing at the Y. As she approaches, you see a black silk scarf. It's long and it plays with her to the rhythm of inaudible music. You don't recognize it; you do recognize her.

Maestro, good evening. I never thought I'd see you in these shadowy places.

You don't answer. You look at her: she's overly made-up, like a woman already, an adult; she's not the student you once knew, and you can almost imagine an extensive life history. She traps you with the scarf, tosses it over you, and you feel the band of cloth on your back. She comes closer to you with a slight pull—a grouping of sets, whole numbers, Samira is equal to—standing, she curls up into you.

Maestro, I like this too much . . . With every man I relive the nights with El Gato, my cat. It's like this dead man comes back to life every day, like a miracle, and I want to do this for the rest of my life. Don't give me that face; I'm happy, and my mom knows all about it—she brought me here. She got laid off at work, like they throw out the trash, that's how they got rid of her. My mom brought me to these dark places and I enjoyed it from the very first time. I couldn't let my little mother go hungry after all that she's done for me, so I closed my eyes and felt my cat on top of me, beside me, and behind me. I also want you to know that for as long as I can remember, after working all day, Mom helped me with my homework at night, we played together, and I went to bed early with a prayer to God. Later, I sometimes escaped from my bed, and would find her with other men in the house. At first she told me it was Daddy who came in spirit to visit her, because spirits have needs too, and at first I believed it, but then I saw Daddy as a big man, other times as a small man. Sometimes he was white, sometimes black, and a few times I saw him with Asian eyes; being a spirit gives you such powers, you can change shape. Some nights Daddy could transform himself into a rich or a poor man, and his soul is so powerful that my mom said it can even transform itself into a woman. And I pretended to believe her. Maestro, I don't want to go back to school. What I wish for now is to be on one of those cheap motel beds, where you can hear people jabbering in the streets, where the red lights change the color of your face, where not even a fan can evaporate my sweat and filth—our filth. Ay, maestro, you don't know how much I've fantasized about you! I've imagined it so many ways that sometimes I think it's real, more real than the men who've been fucking me these past few weeks. Maestro, if you say anything or if I find out that people from the government have done anything to my mom, I swear that you'll never forget me, because I'll tell everyone the story of how you tried to touch me at school. I'll tell them that a few days later you took me on your desk and threatened my grades so you could screw me every day. I'll cry when I tell it, with an expression of shame and pain, and there won't be a single police officer or judge who won't be moved. Ah, I want to go to bed—

You finally escape from the restraint of the scarf and your forehead feels sweaty, your face is hot, and your ears are red. You leave Samira in the darkness and run to the train. *I'm a delinquent,* you think, seeing the terminal as an impossible goal. Finally, it's there in the distance and you can hear your own heart beating like a drum. It's no longer imaginary music, it's an internal percussion. You want to forget that conversation. You want to get home, shower, and erase the memory of Samira's words. You long to be in front of the chalkboard. Invertible functions, variable isolations, ratios and proportions. You see a black cat; it moves quietly, without hurry, without worry. The animal turns around to fix its gray eyes on yours. *If it could speak, what would it say to me?* The feline's gaze is challenging, uncomfortable, and intimidating. You look back the way you've come, back to where you left El Gato's girlfriend. Samira, the girl with the mole in the shape of a cockroach on one elbow, an unsolved equation. With a kind of guilty feeling, you decide to go back and solve it.

INSIDE AND OUTSIDE

BY Edmaris Carazo

Old San Juan

"I'm a resident," he said, and removed the piece of paper from the glove box that apparently confirmed it. The officer looked at it, tilted his head like a dog, checked out my legs, looked him in the eye. He showed the officer his perfect teeth and returned the head tilt. I prayed that he didn't catch a whiff of alcohol on our breath.

He looked at the document again . . . "Go ahead," he finally said, holding the paper a couple seconds more before returning it. He didn't believe us. That's what I thought, but maybe it was because Miguel didn't live in Old San Juan. I really wasn't sure where he lived. Yes, there was his father's house in Carolina, where I waited for him that one time in the pickup while he looked for his board. The same house where we shook the sheets in the half-light of a room with the door open and his old man's snores as background music. There was also that empty apartment with nothing but a cot and a refrigerator, a very useful place but not fit to live in. Resident—a resident of Old San Juan—I doubted it more than the officer did. Anyway, deep down, I celebrated his lie.

Old San Juan is like a family member you miss right up

until the moment you see them again. Not a day goes by that you don't show up and wonder what's going on now, what caused the hullabaloo this time. Then certain streets get shut down and only people who live there can enter. The guards stop you in front of Plaza Colón and filter out those who can enter. The residents of Old San Juan are the lucky ones, those mythical creatures. Nobody knows where they park, or how they're able to go in and out and lead relatively normal lives within the walled city.

The only thing worse than trying to get into Old San Juan on a Friday night is trying to do so when it's raining. On this island, cars stop moving when the first raindrop hits. Any street, any intersection, any checkpoint can become a traffic jam. San Juan in the rain is a spectacle: every puddle illuminated by streetlights, every cobblestone slick—even the disgusting ditches acquire a certain charm. I love cities in the rain. They're like men in suits. If a city doesn't look beautiful in the rain, it never will.

I always enter through the lower end, not caring where I'm going. Even though I come down Avenida Muñoz Rivera as if to go past, I always stop in Plaza Colón, traffic jam or not. I head down as if I were going to the Tapia theater, along the touristy cultural route. I always park at the Doña Fela parking garage on Calle Comercio. It's dark and ugly, but it only costs three dollars for the whole night and it's close to my usual haunts—the restaurants, the bars, Paseo la Princesa. When it's up to me, I stick with Calle Fortaleza and Tetuán. Familiar routes soothe my soul.

I hate driving. When you first start driving, your car is a window of freedom, providing the illusion of being able to go wherever you want—ignoring the small fact that we're stuck on a piece of dirt surrounded by water. Besides, I've been nearsighted since I was twelve, before my first period. At night the lights blind me, and alcohol makes it even worse, drying out my eyes and contacts. My lenses reflect the glare of the stoplights and head-lights of other cars, and the additional $134 was too much to pay to have them put on antireflective coating. It seemed like a pointless charge at the time.

Miguel loves to drive, I imagine in his mind it's like surfing on dry land. Miguel does everything with grace: even scratching his beard, tying his hair up in a bun—that would be feminine if it wasn't for his huge hairy hands filled with rings. Being natural is easy for him, which sounds redundant, but it's not. I, on the other hand, look like I'm about to have an aneurysm when I'm driving through Old San Juan, dodging bums who cross the streets as if they have license plates of their own. It's like they wear dark colors on purpose, blending into the wet cobblestones with their filthy faces and bags on their feet. Maybe that's why I prefer that someone else drives, why I don't question the white lie. Because it saves me from parking in the Doña Fela, allows me to avoid the aroma of rancid piss, of local beer, that sweet rotten smell that fills the city. When I leave the Fela, I usually head right for the street, even though the park-ing lot has a pedestrian walkway. I hurry out through that little exit, "home" to a commune of who knows how many. I don't know if they're the same ones or if they sleep in shifts. I never ever look them in the eye, I dodge their sores, I hold my breath when they're close by. For some reason I have nightmares about passing through that space—I'm terrified that they'll latch onto my legs, throw me to the ground, touch me, infect me.

We got on the Norzagaray and drove around aimlessly, seeing the coast from the highest point on the street, passing by La Perla, like tourists, at a distance—seeing the little colorful houses, crammed together, dropping down to the shore. In its beginnings, La Perla was a slaughterhouse, cemetery, and residence for slaves and servants. It was there that they slaughtered cattle and buried humans, outside the walled city, of course. The poor sometimes have the best views in the world, as well as some cemeteries.

We found a place to park on the street, a miracle that would've never happened to me, and we went down the San Justo hill. Whoever says *bajando hasta las calabazas* obviously hasn't tried to walk down cobblestone in high heels. I was using Miguel as a walker, avoiding cracks, gutters, and raised cobblestones. We stopped at a door, Miguel took out his cell phone, waited, looked up, then down at the ground. "Caballo, I'm outside," he said, and closed the cell phone. It was an old flip phone, prepaid like a burner. While we waited, he hugged me from behind, bit my neck, and squeezed me, until someone appeared in the doorway.

It was a kid—he looked like a minor—pale, bright-eyed, fragile, freshly bathed. "Come in, come in." We followed him up a spiral staircase that seemed endless. It was very dark and smelled like damp wood and cat piss. We came to a huge door, which wasn't a standard rectangle. It was tall, and the upper part was a semicircle with gold-stained glass windows. When it opened, we were transported to another dimension.

It was cold in Old San Juan in mid-August, central air blew throughout the whole world of that apartment, which was covered in varnished wood paneling. The ceilings were exceedingly high; I couldn't help but wonder how the hell they'd hung all those chandeliers. The kitchen was spacious, with stainless-steel appliances. On the other side was the living room, some white leather sofas, plush cushions, and about half a dozen women who looked like they'd been pulled out of the pages of magazines. The music seemed to be coming from the walls themselves. It was one of those electronic rhythms that make the floor and your ribs shake. There were three open bottles of champagne in silver buckets full of ice. And yet, almost nobody was drinking; everyone was dancing, moving their blond heads from side to side, as if hearing a different rhythm.

Migue brought me a glass. I took a breath and put on a questioning face. He kissed me. "Don't ask, just dance."

I drank that champagne with such thirst that it was like I'd walked all the way from the Doña Fela to that strange mansion. I was hoping to feel what everyone else seemed to be feeling, but nothing was happening. I went up to the champagne buffet and filled my glass again. Migue spoke with the kid, while his feline eyes slid over the bodies of the girls. The music had a robotic feel, like a scratched disc, a broken and repetitive melody that gave me more of a headache than a desire to dance. But the rest of the girls danced, eyes closed, fingering their lustrous necklines, smiling as if something very pleasurable was happening to them.

I went back to the table, filled my glass, took three sips, and served myself more. I touched one of the girls on the forearm to get her attention. To my surprise, she opened her big green eyes, smiled, and looked at me as if my face was the most striking one in the world. "Do you know where the bathroom is?" She smiled and tilted her head, came even closer to me, furrowed her brow, and pulled me to her ear—she smelled like lavender and cherry blossoms. "Where's the bathroom?"

"I'll show you."

She turned around, went to the sofa, and began to move the cushions, as if she'd lost something of great value. She went to the other sofa and did the same thing, pushing the cushions aside, sticking her hands into the cracks. Finally, she pulled out a small bag, white and gold, approached me, and took me by the hand. I followed her down a long, dark hallway. It was full of huge canvases, colorful paintings framed in sequoia. I knew the exact kind of wood, because my grandfather had owned a framing business and I spent many summers haggling with galleries and rich people who wanted their recently purchased paintings in frames made of the most expensive material on the market. Then I started to wonder who these people were, who this apartment belonged to, how anyone had so much money in an economy that was so fucked. How old was that kiddo living the life of an artist? Who were these women?

The girl led me to the bathroom and held onto my hand as she entered. She flipped on the light, and I turned to leave. "You can stay."

I smiled at her and looked down at the floor. I think I said, "Thanks," and left. Halfway down the hallway, I remembered I still had to pee. I turned back toward the bathroom, praying to run into the blonde in the hallway. But no, I got back to the bathroom and the door was still shut. Then, as if by magic, it suddenly opened. The blonde threw her head forward as if she was going to kiss her knees, then straightened up quickly. Her hair fell back in a cascade, the image of a mermaid. Her eyes were so big, her eyebrows so high, her lips so red, her smile so wide, so drunk, her jaw set as if fighting an overbite and an underbite at the same time. She went strutting off down the hallway, like she didn't even see me.

I went into the bathroom—I've always thought you can tell everything about a house from the bathroom, like you can tell everything about a man from his shoes. I sat down on the toilet and inspected the room. It resembled a steel urn. It had one of those special showers, the kind you only see in hotels and spas. I looked at myself in the mirror; my eyeliner had run a little and my eyes looked sunken. I attempted to fix it with my fingers but it was a futile effort, so I just pinched my cheeks to give myself a false blush.

When I returned to the living room, I tried to serve myself more champagne. The first two bottles were already empty, so I emptied the third into my glass. "Let's go when you finish that." Miguel didn't fit in that environment either, we looked like we'd been photoshopped in. The chandeliers on the ceiling were reflected in his plastic lenses. He held the glass with both hands, one on the base and the other on the stem, tapping his rings against it. Champagne bubbles are fatal for a beer drinker. Only half of his hair was tied up in a bun. I laughed and told him that we had the same hairdo, touching his hair and scratching his beard. "Let's get out of here." With that whisper, I could tell that Migue had bad intentions, and more alcohol in his body than he knew how to handle.

We put our glasses down on the table and went to say goodbye. Migue grabbed my hand, which was strange. We weren't a handholding couple—we weren't a couple, period. We went down the spiral staircase—which, thanks to the champagne, seemed like the swirling of a giant toilet—and right out onto the cobblestones, this time heading up the San Justo hill. I asked Migue to stop for a second, the ties on my espadrilles had come undone. He stopped, crouched down, and tied them for me with all the calm and care in the world. I had no idea what time it was.

"Whose apartment is that?"

"Well, it's Julito's."

"No, but who does it belong to?"

"I already told you."

"Migue, that kid is like seventeen."

"Nineteen."

"And what does he do?"

"He manages."

"It must come from his family then—what do his parents do?"

"Dunno, they've got an art gallery or something."

He got all gallant and opened the pickup door for me. I could barely climb in, it's too high for my short legs, and champagne doesn't typically make you more skilled at anything.

"Are you good to drive?" I asked.

"Sure."

We turned onto one of the little streets, Luna or Sol, I always confuse them. But we kept ascending.

"Aren't we going?" I was confused.

"Yes."

He pulled over to the side of the road, and started texting. I began looking all around, it seemed like we were just waiting to be mugged. Soon, a bum appeared, with a backpack, shorts, infinite beard, and bare feet. Migue rolled down the window. I'd seen him roll down the window other times to give them money, or tell them to find some shoes in the back of his truck. *Oh, Migue, not today.*

The guy opened the door, removed his backpack, got in the pickup, settled in, shut the door, and greeted us. Migue locked the doors and put his hand on my thigh, as if telling me to stay calm. He took a manila envelope out of the glove box. The guy pulled a package from his backpack, a brick wrapped in plastic. He set it down between my seat and Migue's. Migue picked it up, unwrapped it, and pulled out a heavy green brick. I couldn't believe it, it was like a bar of gold, but it was weed.

They shook hands, and the guy slipped the manila envelope in his backpack and said, "Buenas noches, miss." And he got out.

"Sorry you had to be here for this," Miguel said

"Sorry? You know the position you put me in?"

"You know I—"

"That you smoke weed, like all the time? Yes. Did I expect you to deal drugs with me in the car? No!"

"It's no big thing."

"Start the car, let's go. And don't take me around San Juan doing stupid shit, I need you to bring me home, and that's it."

There were cops diverting traffic in the middle of San Juan. On the other side, the streets are one-ways. So we ended up taking the longest way around—not along the coast, not by the docks, but in the interior. We went right through the intestines of the old city.

The silence in the car was almost as tempestuous as the music in that mansion apartment. Migue fiddled with the air-conditioning, trying to defog the windows. It had rained most of the night and the city was damp, cold, and foggy. He had let his hair down, and he drove with his right hand while resting his head on his left. When we got out of the walled city, the only noise was our breathing and the swoosh of the tires over the wet tar. Free of the cobblestones, at last we could move at a decent speed.

I looked out my window as we moved away from Old San Juan and returned to the city like the rest of the mortals. I was more sad than angry about what had happened. Migue was generally a good guy, and many times I'd wondered if our thing was going somewhere. I was savoring the journey without destination that we were on, and his hands always made me happy, so I enjoyed the coming and going without thinking of dates or reasons. But what had happened that day was forcing me to make a decision, to draw lines, define things—the opposite of everything we were.

I heard a deep gasp, as if Migue were reading my mind. I turned to look at him and his brow furrowed. He pushed back from the steering wheel to plant himself in the seat and stretched out his right arm as if he could protect me from flying out the windshield. The world was moving in slow motion. I felt a violent lurch and almost hit the dashboard. The screeching of tires broke the silence. When I managed to look up, I saw the silhouette of a man, then the details of his face growing clearer—coming closer and closer, as if focusing binoculars—until I could recognize the panic in his eyes, and then the impact came. I closed my eyes. I still heard the screech of the tires and the impact, again and again, pulsing from jaw to sternum. I opened my eyes and looked at Migue. He didn't have his glasses on, and he was covering his face with his hands with their many rings. "What do I do? What do I do? WHAT DO I DO!" He ran his hands over his forehead and pushed his hair back, over and over. When I dared to look out the windshield, I saw the body on the ground. It was wet and his face was looking in the other direction. His clothes were dark. It was impossible to know whether or not he was breathing. Migue unfastened his seat belt and unlocked the doors.

"What're you doing?"

"I've gotta take him to the hospital."

"Miguel, you're crazy."

"We can't just leave him lying there."

"You know how much we had to drink?"

"What's that got to do with it?"

"We could go to jail, Miguel."

"No way, it was an accident."

"An accident? If we're unlucky enough to have killed the bum, it's like homicide, Migue, seriously."

"What does it matter that he's a bum?"

"He's got no family, nobody's gonna give two shits about investigating. Start the car, let's go."

"I can't do that, I can't."

"We drank a ton and we're driving around with a brick of marijuana in the car, we don't have any other option."

Miguel looked down. He tied his hair into a half-bun, dried his tears, crossed himself, and started the car.

Pedestrian Run Over in Old San Juan

At 4:23 a.m. yesterday, there was a report of a serious accident involving a pedestrian. The incident took place on Avenida Constitución at the exit of the walled city, in the jurisdiction of the municipality of San Juan.

According to the preliminary report, the incident occurred when a vehicle, described as a blue pickup, was driving down the aforementioned roadway toward Avenida Ponce de León. Several neighbors in the vicinity said that the female driver abandoned the scene immediately.

The body of the victim was identified as Julio Botet, owner of the Galería Éxodo on Calle San Francisco in Old San Juan.

Agent Nicholás Marrero of the Highway Patrol Division of the Puerto Rican Police Command at Avenida Fernández Juncos Station, Parada 6 in Puerta de Tierra, and District Attorney Esteban Mendizábal have taken charge of the investigation, ordering that the scene be photographed and analyzed.

DEATH ANGEL OF SANTURCE

BY CHARLIE VÁZQUEZ

Avenida Fernández Juncos

She has dyed blond hair that's turned orange in spots, and her eyes twitch left and right as she storms down Avenida Fernández Juncos in a panic. Her red blouse should be tighter and she pulls her short black skirt up as she goes. Of medium complexion—not white, not black—she was once very beautiful.

Shattered glass crunches under her scuffed maroon heels as she passes windows that are barred like prison cells—or tiger cages—along the restless Santurce thoroughfare on the night that will claim her forever. She knows something's wrong, very wrong, and fears that she'll never find her way out again.

So she runs to him in the meantime.

The tantalizing aroma of a pig being fire-roasted whole for a celebration floats past her on the pirate breezes that sneak in like thieves from the brooding Atlantic Ocean. The breezes always disappear inland, toward the lush, mysterious green mountains in the dark island interior.

She forgets her hunger as soon as the winds move on and now she won't stop for anything. Only one thing haunts her thoughts tonight and she will not cease until he appears. She digs through her purse and sprays her neck and armpits with a flowery perfume she stole from a pharmacy.

I've missed him, she thinks, and snaps her compact closed, wedging it between her lips in order to undo and redo her frizzy ponytail, tighter and cleaner. She hurries down the dark avenue as cars zoom past blasting salsa, and the descendants of shipwrecked derelicts linger, drinking liquor out of brown papers bags.

They lick their lips and call her precious things. A man appears out of nowhere in a green tank top and dirty blue jeans. He's tall, dark, and smells of beer; a lightning flash of pink tongue sneaks out, pornographic desire.

"Hey, mami, come over here—"

"Go to hell, cabrón!" she says, and shoves him out of the way.

The man keeps talking to her—he trails her for an entire block—and his voice fades away with the now distant, distorted pulse of salsa in the background. She quickens her pace, careful not to misjudge the uneven pavement beneath her throbbing feet. She has to avoid injury tonight; no distractions or accidents this time.

Our young lady of the night wonders what time it is (a constant concern since her watch and cell phone were stolen), as she passes a loud parade of whistling and catcalling men who grope themselves and conspire to slow her down—or stop her. She breaks through them and continues on her quest, not stopping to ask for the hour.

Specters linger under the swaying shadows of palms draped in moonless darkness, like something out of one of those old black-and-white movies her grandfather used to love. Her mother would pass the day watching them when she was a little girl, and now she adores them too.

A familiar outline materializes in the darkness up ahead. It becomes clearer and approaches with threatening speed: another young woman working the same perilous trade approaches, her black eyes and sculpted eyebrows narrowed and pinched tightly with confrontation. Her hair and outfit are Gothic black and she curls her dagger-filed fingernails into her fists with feline grace. "You got some nerve—"

"You got nothing and I got a date, puta," our young lady tells her. "Now, get out of my way before I kill you." She pushes the newcomer aside and digs through her purse for a knife, almost knocking the cat-girl off her feet. Their throaty profanities echo off the buildings and ricochet over the busy avenue, and men passing in cars press down on their horns excitedly. One fellow stops and offers to take them both with him.

Our young lady of the night ignores him—that motherfucker doesn't have any money—and finishes telling the cat-bitch what she's been waiting to tell her for some time. Then she puts her knife away and continues on her aching feet, letting the puta live for now.

Hissing, cat-girl fades away from the frame as she approaches the man in the driver's seat—"Wait for me, papi," she says—as his friends in the backseat deepen their voices and squash together to make room for her. They grasp the heads of their dicks through their basketball shorts and the salsa pulse gets louder.

She resumes her frantic journey through the treasonous streets and thinks she'll need to charge him more money from now on. She can already see the surprise and hurt in his old brown eyes, which always stare at her from somewhere long ago and far away, from another place in time.

Always a gentleman, and still handsome for an old dog, he pays her in crisp hundred-dollar bills he sometimes counts incorrectly in her favor. If the moon is right, he'll even take her to a fancy Old San Juan restaurant and let her spend the night in his expensive hotel, after putting his valuables in the safe and taking his teeth out.

He never asks for kinky or freaky tricks (she wishes he would for a change), or says things to upset and degrade her for his pleasure—unlike so many losers. Those rich losers who get off on the suffering of others. He's easier to turn over than men half his age, and she's had him figured out for over a year.

Our young lady of the night arrives at the designated tavern—*Finally,* she sighs as she enters—and orders a can of Medalla. It's all she can afford until he arrives. She waits near his favorite seat, gulping her beer and listening to a new bachata hit.

He's over twenty minutes late, which is unlike him. She rummages through her purse, unsure of what she's looking for. *He better not be dead.*

She has no phone, but that doesn't matter since the old man's married and always calls from a blocked number. She asks the meaty-armed bartender if her date has been around, describing him, and the bartender tells her no. She writes something on a piece of paper and passes it to him.

A second and then a third Medalla appear, followed by several shots of vodka. Our young lady of the night hasn't eaten dinner, but she doesn't care because she's never coming back here—she's finished with this place, this infernal island of heartache, this city she used to love.

Her aunt Yolanda in Philadelphia will be happy to have her visit, and after that—she says to herself as the meaty-armed bartender sets a fifth Medalla down—she'll go to Florida because she hates the snow. Snow is for gringo motherfuckers. Twice in her short life was enough.

The bartender stops serving her when the overweight, sweaty owner comes in to catch up on some office business in the back with an attractive young woman. He winks, hands her four squashed Marlboro Reds, and tells her it's time to get moving.

"Come meet me tomorrow around midnight," he says. "I get paid and . . ."

She stumbles out, doesn't answer him.

Over two hours late. This has never happened before. She gives up and says a prayer for him. She knows it'll do nothing, but she doesn't know what else to do. The night brings answers to every question. It always has and why should tonight be any different?

Our young lady of the night passes even more people on her way home than she had on the way to her ruined date. Shadows and silhouettes appear to ask her things

(*Are they really there?* she wonders), and she waves them off and sucks her teeth with disgust. She'll be living on the streets again soon, so fuck them and their problems.

The next time that ugly old motherfucker wants a date, I'll make him pay double, she laughs in the haze and warmth of silly intoxication. She considers going back to the clubs to make some last-minute money, but she was banned from all of them for stealing. A lie. Another lie.

Our young lady digs around in her purse and lights a cigarette with shaky hands. Then she pulls out two wrinkled school photos of her little man—her little boy, her little prince—who lives in Ponce with his asshole father. The motherfucker who kicked her out to marry that bitch, the reason for all of this . . .

She puts her hands to her face. The convulsive bursts of emotion rock her. The shameful agony of not having her son with her explodes from her core, and she kneels on the pavement, using a parked car to keep balance, until it passes several moments later. People walk right past, as if she isn't even there.

I'll get my little man back, she thinks, but it's just as hard when he's around. So she stops at the entrance of an avocado-green apartment building where she cannot be seen and lets the last stabs of hoarse anguish drain out. This passes too, and she blows her nose into a napkin she finds in her purse.

Lights another cigarette.

At least you aren't dead, she says to herself, hooking her bag on her shoulder.

Tomorrow's her birthday; it's only one in the morning, and she feels like celebrating. There's no one around to tell her she can't. Our young lady of the night walks past another bar and tries her luck. *Why not?* Even a glass of water would be good. She's cried all the moisture out of her body and another drink will help her forget for a while.

She steps aside to inspect herself in her broken compact one final time and approves of the reflection, despite another missing tooth, blotting away the trails of makeup from her tears. She walks in and sucks up her runny nose, a blast of marijuana smoke hitting her nostrils.

There's a loud, awful heavy metal ballad playing that she remembers from an MTV video when she spent her summers in Philadelphia as a little girl. Ugly gringo motherfuckers in women's clothes and makeup with long nasty hair, and endless guitar solos that would drive a deaf person crazy. They're not the Stones, that's for sure.

Our young lady of the night wants a man, one who'll hold her after he's done. She spots a muscular guy wearing a chunky watch and gold chains sitting alone at the bar, typing something into his phone. Her favorite Santo Boricua tank-top physique. He's handsome as a jaguar and looks like he has money to spend.

She introduces herself and brightens when she smells his sweat, but then a curly haired, high-heeled Dominican woman slams the squeaky bathroom door behind her, walks up to our young lady of the night— her perfume is too strong—and pushes her out of the way.

"What the fuck are you doing talking to my man, puta?"

"The only puta you need to be worried about is your mother," our young lady says, and lunges to grab her hair.

They scream insults at one another, pushing as the boyfriend with rocky muscles and black armpit hair tries to break them apart.

"Stop that shit, puñeta!" he says.

They stumble apart and our young lady of the night gets ready to leave before things get too hot. She's too drunk to fight. The Dominican woman continues to call her a list of horrible things; her man is embarrassed and finishes his beer, swipes his car keys off the bar to leave.

He's ready to fuck, the lonely woman thinks; she can see it in his walk and hear it in his voice. She savors the thought of him taking her—he's the kind of man she would keep around—but he disappears into the night, keeping his girl calm at his side as he does.

There's an older guy there but she's had enough of them. He's at the back of the bar and is dressed like a leading man from an old black-and-white movie. Staring down at something—a magazine? His phone? She can't see his face.

Something pulls her to him, so she stumbles over and tells him her name, that she thinks she's seen him before. He doesn't look up but nods without the slightest degree of emotion or interest—this overdressed man from an old movie.

He gestures with an open palm for her to sit, which she does, but he still doesn't say anything or even look up. He mumbles something she doesn't understand in a smooth, deep voice she finds pleasant. She suspects he is lonely like she is, and waits for him to meet her gaze or say something, offer her a drink.

He raises his head after a few tense moments and she gasps. He's not old at all. What was she thinking? He's one of the most handsome men she's ever seen: friendly, penetrating blue eyes, combed-back silver hair, with about three days' worth of a stubbly beard.

Our young lady feels dizzy when she smells his fresh, piney cologne. He undoes the top two buttons of his crisp white shirt to reveal thick chest hair. No wedding ring. *Well-groomed and elegant*, she thinks. *Easy in bed*.

Suddenly she is overcome by a terrible feeling and tells herself that it's best to get moving and go home where she can lock the door and get away from the world. She's drunk and it's best to leave before something awful happens.

He's so handsome that she cannot look at him for too long.

The stylish devil leans over and says something. His voice is dry and reptilian, yet familiar, and she nods in approval at everything he says. They leave the bar—and the terrible heavy metal music—and head to her room just a few blocks from there, making a quick stop along the way.

She leads him into the dark lobby and up an even darker staircase to her room. The building is without power, she tells him, but they can take a cold shower to freshen up from the humid night.

He remains silent and enters after her. She lights

candles for atmosphere, romance—so they can see one another—and excuses herself to the bathroom to wash up for several anxious and jittery minutes, before emerging anew.

Glowing.

Naked.

He's sitting in the corner, still dressed, and she wonders how she could've mistaken him for an ugly old monster. He won't take his clothes off, he says, because he's not staying. He works nights and has a lot to do. *Another freak*, she thinks, *but at least he smells nice. And he looks strong. Maybe he'll even hold me.*

She wonders what'll turn him on as she leads him to her bed. She lies on her back in the storm of her intoxication and he falls on top of her, crashing down and spreading her legs apart. A wooden bedpost creaks and splinters and he hushes her with a finger to her lips when she tries to say something.

He unbuckles his belt, unzips his suit pants, pulls it out, and guides it into her. Their desire ignites and launches her to strange and wonderful worlds—to new realms where everything is fantastic and wondrous. She lets out long, throaty animal sounds that mean many prophetic things in the moment, but he says nothing.

Our young lady of the night rocks her head left and right in ecstasy: there's a handsome man on top of her, dressed exquisitely and smelling of expensive cologne; no foul body odors, or sore spots, or careful maneuvering around broken bones and bandages.

He moans into her ear and she spreads wider for him, his prong swelling wider inside her. It hurts, because it has a sharp curve and is thicker than her wrists, so she shifts her hips to makes it easier, to take him all the way in.

He grinds into her, burying his snout into the space just below her ear. She feels teeth push against her neck, harder each time. Something overcomes him and he sinks his teeth into her shoulder, piercing her skin. He thrusts harder at the taste of her blood.

Our young lady screams in protest, but his hand is over her mouth. His charming cologne becomes foul and cadaverous, and each of his movements chips away at her strength. His fingers become sharp claws that tear her flesh off the bone, and her eyes light up with the screams that are silenced in her throat. In tandem with his cruel teeth, they rip her body to shreds.

She screams one final plea and loses consciousness. Deafening hurricane winds shatter the windows, and the dissonant groans of the resurrected dead rush in on the trade winds.

The curtains become still.

The nervous hotel manager explains that the power hasn't been restored yet as he puts his heavy key ring back in his pocket and opens the door. The first officer enters, pinches his nose. The second follows with instinctive hesitation. The dirty manager, a chubby and religious middle-aged man, lingers behind and says a prayer.

It's been days since anyone's heard from her. A young woman who disguised her voice and lied about her identity was the one to alert the police that something was wrong. The hotel manager explains to the cops that she's five months behind on her rent. "Always has money for everything else, if you know what I mean."

The officers ignore him. They've heard it all and they know what they're doing. It's as humid as it gets in San Juan and they're dressed in their black uniforms. The stench in the room doesn't help much, but it solves the mystery.

She's faceup in bed; legs spread wide; an angelic and peaceful expression on her darkening face. Her left arm is tossed aside, punctured with agony and guilt. Skin spotting over. Her makeup's smeared and streaked, as if she'd been crying.

"Everything else looks fine," the officers say to one another. The only unusual detail is her eyes, which are open wide with wonder, as if the last thing she'd seen had been astonishing and beautiful.

"You thinking what I'm thinking?" the younger cop asks.

The older cop curtly tells him to cover her body with the blanket, as if insulted by his stupid question, and is-sues a report over his radio. He tells the manager he can start cleaning the place up, that she doesn't have much and what's there is worthless. As if she were still alive.

He goes through her purse and finds two photos of a little boy that resembles her. He wedges them into the corners of a framed image of the Virgin Mary that hangs next to the locked window. Shakes his head.

"No sign of a break-in or any other disturbance," he says to the dispatcher. "No need to send Detective Guer-rero since there's nothing to investigate. Overdose."

The hotel manager steps back and the officers continue. The older cop hands her purse to the younger one to look through (no money, no credit cards) and checks the locked window one last time. Then he goes into the bathroom and comes out with a curled-over tablespoon and syringe and throws them onto the bed next to her.

He shoots a small plastic baggie into the air with a flick of his middle finger and says, "Another satisfied customer."

"She probably scored on Fernández Juncos, overestimated the dose, and well . . ." the younger officer says with a hint of sadness in his voice.

"You know everything already, don't you?" the older one says.

The electricity comes on and the television whines back to life. A weak lightbulb flickers on overhead and an old movie brightens to life on the screen. The younger officer crosses the room to switch it off. *This nasty old hotel actually has cable*, he thinks, and takes in the moving image of a pretty woman jumping into an elegant man's arms for a brief moment.

"At least she had good enough taste to watch old black-and-white movies," he says to the grumpy senior officer. The image darkens with a metallic ringing sound when he turns the TV off. "Because the new ones suck."

Originally written in English

ABOUT THE CONTRIBUTORS

Johanny Becerra

JANETTE BECERRA is a fiction, poetry, and essay writer. She has published two volumes of short stories (*Ciencia imperfecta* and *Doce versiones de soledad*), two poetry books (*La casa que soy* and *Elusiones*), and a children's novel (*Antrópolis*). Her creative and critical work has been published in Venezuela, Cuba, Denmark, Spain, Portugal, and Tunisia. She holds a PhD in Spanish literature from the University of Puerto Rico, where she has taught since 2000.

Huáscar Robles

WILFREDO J. BURGOS MATOS is a singer, journalist, and writer from Puerto Rico living in New York. He has been published in the main newspapers on the island and is the president of Proyecto Educativo y Cultural Unidad Insular (PECUI), an initiative that offers creative writing workshops in the Dominican Republic and Puerto Rico. He's currently completing a PhD at the Graduate Center, CUNY, where he is researching Caribbean music in its transnational context.

Gabriel René Rodríguez

EDMARIS CARAZO has maintained a blog, *siemprejueves.blogspot.com*, since 2008. Her short story "En Temporada" was published in the *Cuentos de Oficio: Anthology of Emerging Storytellers in Puerto Rico*, and she won an honorable mention in the 2013 Novel Contest of the Institute of Culture of Puerto Rico with her manuscript *El Día que me venció el olvido*. Currently, Carazo works as a digital communications manager at an advertising agency.

Miguel Zayas

TERE DÁVILA is author of two story collections: *Lego y otros pájaros raros* and *El fondillo maravilloso y otros efectos especiales*. Her award-winning stories have been published in Spanish and English anthologies: *Latitud 18.5, El ojo del huracán, Cuentos puertorriqueños para el nuevo milenio,* and *Palabras: Dispatches from the Festival de la Palabra*. She has a BA from Harvard University and a master's degree in creative writing. Dávila lives in San Juan and is finishing her first novel.

Miguel Marín-Fuster

ANA MARÍA FUSTER LAVÍN is a Puerto Rican writer and cultural columnist. She has received awards from the PEN chapter in Puerto Rico for her novel *Réquiem*, and from El Instituto de Literatura Puertorriqueña for her story collection *Verdades caprichosas*. She is also the author of numerous poetry collections, including *El libro de las sombras, Tras la sombra de la luna,* and *El eróscopo;* and the gothic novel *(In)somnio*.

MANUEL A. MELÉNDEZ was born in Puerto Rico and raised in East Harlem, New York. He is the author of two novels, four poetry collections, and two collections of short stories. His novel *Battle for a Soul* was a finalist for the 2015 International Latino Book Award for Best Mystery Novel. He's currently working on a collection of suspenseful short stories as well as a mystery novel, and lives in Sunnyside, New York.

LUIS NEGRÓN, a writer and bookseller, was born in Guayama, Puerto Rico, in 1970. *Mundo cruel* (2010), his first book, was awarded, in its English translation, with a 2013 Lambda Literary Award. His work has being adapted for the theater and cinema.

MANOLO NÚÑEZ NEGRÓN studied Latin American literature at the University of Puerto Rico–Río Piedras, and earned a PhD from Harvard. He was an assistant professor at Wellesley College, Massachusetts. Currently, he teaches at the University of Puerto Rico–Río Piedras. His first book of short stories, *El oficio del vértigo*, was published in 2010. In 2012 he published his first novella, *Barra china*.

ALEJANDRO ÁLVAREZ NIEVES is a Puerto Rican writer and translator, and an adjunct professor at the Graduate Program in Translation at the University of Puerto Rico–Río Piedras. He completed a PhD in translation studies from Universidad de Salamanca in 2013. His short stories have been published in several journals and publications. His poetry book *El proceso traductor* won the *El Nuevo Día* Poetry Contest in 2011.

YOLANDA ARROYO PIZARRO is a Puerto Rican writer. Her story collection *Las negras* won the National Prize from the PEN chapter in Puerto Rico in 2013. She has also won awards from the Institute of Puerto Rican Culture in 2012 and 2015, and from El Instituto de Literatura Puertorriqueña in 2008. Her notable children's books include *La Linda Señora Tortuga* and *Thiago y la aventura de los túneles de San Germán*.

Scarlet Quiñonez

ERNESTO QUIÑONEZ was heralded by the *Village Voice* as a "Writer on the Verge." The *New York Times* called his debut novel *Bodega Dreams* a "new immigrant classic." It has since become a landmark in contemporary American literature and is required reading in many colleges around the country. He is a Sundance Writer's Lab fellow and is currently an associate professor at Cornell University's MFA program.

Laura Rabelo

JOSÉ RABELO is a Puerto Rican writer and dermatologist. He graduated from the University of Puerto Rico Medical Sciences program and received his master's degree in creative writing from the Universidad del Sagrado Corazón. He won the National Prize for Children's Stories in 2003 for his story collection *Cielo, mar y tierra*. He is the author of three novels: *Cartas a Datovia, Los sueños ajenos,* and *Azábara*. He received the Premio El Barco de Vapor in 2013 for *Club de calamidades*.

Adal Maldonado

MAYRA SANTOS-FEBRES has published more than twenty-five books of poetry, short stories, essay collections, and novels. Among her most well-known titles are *Sirena Selena* (2000), *Our Lady of the Night* (2006), and *La amante de Gardel* (2015). In 1996 she won the Juan Rulfo Award for her short story "Oso blanco." Her works have been translated into Croatian, Icelandic, French, Italian, German, and English. She currently teaches creative writing at the University of Puerto Rico.

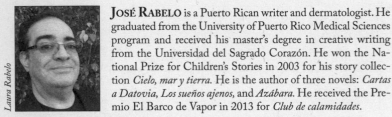

Luisa Rivera

WILL VANDERHYDEN is a translator of Spanish-language literature. He has an MA in literary translation from the University of Rochester. He has translated two novels by the Chilean writer Carlos Labbé, *Navidad & Matanza* and *Loquela*, for Open Letter Books. His translations have appeared in journals like the *Literary Review, Asymptote*, and *Two Lines*. In 2015, he received an NEA Translation Fellowship and a Lannan Writer's Residency.

Rebecca Beard

CHARLIE VÁZQUEZ is the director of the Bronx Writers Center, as well as the author of the novels *Buzz and Israel* (2005), and *Contraband* (2010). He has served as the New York City coordinator for Puerto Rico's Festival de la Palabra and has just finished his third novel, a paranormal mystery set in Old San Juan. He lives in the Bronx, where he was born.